the storm
is coming

An Anthology

Also available from Sleeping Cat Books

A Dickens Christmas: A Christmas Carol and Other Stories

the storm is coming

AN ANTHOLOGY

EDITED BY SARAH E. HOLROYD

Sleeping Cat
Books

THE STORM IS COMING: AN ANTHOLOGY

Sleeping Cat Books
http://sleepingcatbooks.com

This book is a work of fiction. Names, characters, places, and incidents either are the product of the author's imagination or are used fictitiously. Any resemblance to actual events or locales or persons, living or dead, is entirely coincidental.

Cover design: Sarah E. Holroyd
Interior design: Sarah E. Holroyd

ISBN-13: 978-0984679805
ISBN-10: 0984679804

table of contents

NOTE FROM THE EDITOR

Storms can come out of a clear blue sky, or they can build over a long period. They can take many forms, all terribly destructive: from a tornado or hurricane that can destroy all your belongings, to an abusive spouse who can destroy your sense of well-being, to human actions that can destroy an entire society.

With this collection of short stories, poetry, non-fiction, and images, I've tried to capture the range of approaching storms, and the range of emotions involved in such cataclysmic events. Within these pages you will find Mother Nature on the warpath in the form of tornadoes, hurricanes, blizzards, and vengeful plants. You will find storms approaching in the form of an abusive spouse, a fed-up spouse, and the down-trodden. You will find murder, suicide, and life beginning anew.

I enjoyed the process of creating this collection, and I hope that you will enjoy reading it just as much.

Sarah E. Holroyd

Jazz Arrives at Zorand

WALTON MENDELSON

Walton is a writer, musician, and visual artist living in Arizona. As a colleague of the visual artist Frederick Sommer, he performed and recorded *The Music of Frederick Sommer* (Nazraeli Press). Walton's visual work has been both collaborative (*Metaphysics in Jars*, Nazraeli Press) and solo (*Miscellanea*, One Off Press). His short stories have been published in print and online literary magazines.

Waiting for the Rain

Krikor Der Hohannesian

Krikor Der Hohannesian lives in Medford, MA, and has been writing poetry for some 40 years, though only submitting work over the past several years. Since then, he has had poems published in many literary journals including *The Evansville Review*, *The South Carolina Review*, *Atlanta Review*, *Peregrine*, *The New Renaissance*, *Hawai'i Pacific Review*, and *Connecticut Review*. He has also received honorable mention for the New England Poetry Club's Gretchen Warren Award for best published poem of 2010. His first chapbook, *Ghosts and Whispers*, was published by Finishing Line Press (2010) and has been nominated for the Pen New England and Mass Book Awards. He serves as Assistant Treasurer of the New England Poetry Club.

In the afflicted very young
there is a phrase for it,
"failure to thrive,"
a lack of interest
in their yet small worlds,
a tendency to squall more
than most—not yet have they
the words to describe.

For those of us nearing the inevitable,
the drip, drip of falling energy,
the ache in the bones, the skin
cracking like a dried-up arroyo,
waiting for the gully-washer
that never comes. There is
a catch-all for this, too—
"Ah, it's just old age."

For the aging poet it is words,
his life blood, that slowly dry up.
He searches for rock hibiscus
and pigeon-berry in his desert
of desiccated inspiration. He
hopes for the flood of afternoon rain,
the thunder-squall of words, the poem,
the arc of the rainbow at day's end.

the wait

FARAH GHUZNAVI

Farah Ghuznavi is an international development professional and newspaper columnist. Her fiction has been published in the UK, US, Canada, Singapore, and her native Bangladesh. Anthologies featuring her work include *Woman's Work: Short Stories* (GirlChild Press, US), *The Rainbow Feast* (Marshall Cavendish, Singapore), *Curbside Splendor* Issues 1 and 2 (Curbside Splendor, US), *Journeys* (Sampad, Britain), *What the Ink?* (Writers Block, Bangladesh), *From the Delta* (UPL, Bangladesh), and *The Monster Book for Girls* (Exaggerated Press, UK). Her story "Judgement Day" received Highly Commended in the 2010 Commonwealth Competition, and another story placed second in the Oxford University GEF Competition. Farah is currently editing a fiction anthology for the Indian publisher Zubaan. Her website is: www.farahghuznavi.com.

IT'S HAPPENING AGAIN. A FAMILIAR RAGE UNFOLDS its sticky wings within the captive interior of my chest: a monstrous butterfly emerging gracelessly from its cocoon.

It's the same every night. The taste of panic blooms bitter on my tongue. Swallowing hard, I wonder how much longer I can bear this charade.

I sculpt my features into submissiveness by a sheer act of will, reminding myself sternly that it's only during dinner that I must endure your company. It's the one meal we eat together; indeed, the only time of day that we are even in the same room. I have tapped unexpected creativity to find excuses to wander away after you return home from work, disappearing to the far ends of the house, carefully casual in my movements so as not to attract unwanted attention.

You haven't noticed my reaction now, either. You never do. Spooning your food onto that ridiculous brass platter you insist on using, you proceed to eat it in the familiar, methodical, *maddening* sequence that supposedly provides optimal nutrition. You are obsessed with your health. Now in your fifties, you want to live forever.

Ayurveda has provided the answer, as far as you're concerned. Returning to the ways of our ancestors, you call it. The frugality of the system suits you: an approach both pure and puritanical.

You can spare me the lectures, I know all about it. How many times have you droned on about the principles of food preparation—haranguing me about the spices to be ground and added in specific proportions, which fresh herbs to use for a particular dish, and so on, and so endlessly on.

Thanks to you, I've spent years learning about the medicinal benefits of plants. But time spent gathering knowledge is never wasted. And I have learned more than you will ever know. In fact, I could teach you a few things...

My attention returns unexpectedly to the present, as you actually tell me that something tastes good. But it's too little, too late. I am tired of it all now—of your endless complaints, your chronic self-absorption.

My impatience to get away begins to spiral out of control. Your words are gradually crowded out by the *kalbaisakhi*[1] taking over my brain. Soon, I will hear nothing but the relentless raindrops beating a wild tattoo against my shuttered skull, as I clench my teeth from the effort of keeping the whirling winds of rage at bay.

Unaware of my traitorous thoughts, your lips continue to move. They flap in the quickening breeze, while that insidious inner voice of mine mocks every move you make: your preoccupation with your irregular bowels, your mother's opinions on everything, your brother's financial success that you profess to admire, yet resent so deeply.

When I married you, I was the awkward daughter in my accomplished family. Not academically inclined despite my professorial parentage, nor light-skinned and graceful as we are bludgeoned into believing that an Indian woman should be. More than two decades older, turmeric-stained by the remnants of a failed marriage, you were nevertheless deemed a catch for a girl like me. With neither beauty nor intellect to recommend me, my parents were happy at what they considered a fair exchange: a youthful bride who'd restore your status as a "real man" in return for my guaranteed salvation from the disgrace of potential spinsterhood.

In the beginning, I was too inexperienced to know what to expect. I had merely hoped to escape the smothering weight of doomed parental expectations—to begin living a life of my own, however ordinary. Whatever references I had were drawn from the starry-eyed heroines of the Mills and Boon romances that I was so addicted to. But ten dreary years, the despair of continuous boredom, and three miscarriages later, I have come to realize that this is no Cinderella story. You are hardly a savior. Not even much of a man, really.

I wish I could have just left you. But my parents would never have provided shelter to such a disgraceful daughter, and I had little faith in my own skills; a knowledge of the more arcane aspects of botany hardly counts for much in the modern-day job market.

 No, initiating the departure from my marriage would have

1   A tropical storm full of sound and fury—takes place during storm season in India and Bangladesh in March–April

been an excruciating process—involving a series of post-mortems and recriminations, warnings and wishful thinking about second chances. So I found another way.

You will be the one to leave me, though not just yet. You will die.

Datura and *Aconite* are well-known herbal toxins, but there are many other, more obscure, "witches' weeds" tucked away in the depths of the manuals, awaiting discovery by the discerning scholar. In the end, I found the perfect one.

In tiny doses, *Mitracorum* is undetectable. And highly effective; there are no visible side-effects until the final moments. I can vouch for the truth of those claims. Since I started, you haven't displayed so much as a diminishing of appetite for the "pure-veg" pap that you insist on inflicting on us both, let alone signs of poisoning.

To assuage my fraying patience, all I have to do is dwell on the years of freedom that lie ahead. I am no longer bothered by pangs of conscience—they suffocated long ago under the obese weight of your demands. The benefits of being a too-young bride are now becoming evident to me.

They are further enhanced by your miserly habits, which have guaranteed me a solvent future as your grieving widow. And when that time comes, I will finally be free of those who have for so long controlled my life in the name of respectability. All I need is a little more patience.

The storm will break soon. But I am ready, waiting in my bunker, yearning for its arrival.

Waiting

Danica Green

Danica Green is a UK-based writer with publishing credits in more than thirty anthologies and literary journals. She likes to think her work covers a wide range of genres and ideas but she hasn't quite gotten the hang of writing anything that isn't horribly depressing. She's working on it.

A FLICKERING BULB ILLUMINATED THE KITCHEN SINK,
reflecting off the tarnished silver and gold wedding band wrapped
around a wrinkled finger. Elsie looked to the ceiling and sighed before bending back to the task at hand, scrubbing single-mindedly
to take away the stinging pain felt in red, raw hands. The wind was
getting up outside and she couldn't help but curse the weather for
never bringing snow, that beautiful blanket that covers the world
and hides its sins in soft white purity. The wind and rain were all
that ever came. She knew the snow could only hide what lay underneath, but the rain never washed it away; there was never any sense
of cleansing as the rain would only swill the dirt around and on the
next crisp morning it would lie in piles on the sidewalk, frozen in
lumps, immovable, drawing eyes to its imperfection.

Elsie's eyes wandered to her wedding ring and she snorted softly
through her small nose. The snow would bring its own problems:
the inability to travel, a day spent inside with him yowling like an
angry feline and berating her for not doing the chores she was currently in the middle of.

The wind rose again and clattered against the door. Elsie's eyes
fluttered to the clock above and to the right, then back to the sink as
she redoubled her efforts. The last plate was hauled to the draining
board, dried, and put neatly away in the cupboard, the sink cleaned,
the plug placed precisely on the side. Now was the time of day she
dreaded most, that brief interlude after washing up but before the
oven timer alerted her to remove the roast—ten solitary minutes
of standing still. She cracked her knuckles nervously, eyes dart-
ing, always slightly lost when she wasn't moving, tidying, fulfilling
her purpose. Her mind drifted briefly to television and bookcases,
those magical little time wasters which always seemed to take just
a little longer to start enjoying than her paltry ten minutes allowed.

She walked to the window and opened the curtain with one
chapped finger, the motion causing the dry skin to split along the
nail and trickle blood down across her knuckles. She swore loudly
and ran to the sink, washing the wound and rooting around in
the drawer for a band-aid. The wind thumped again and a distant
growl of thunder caused a tear to spring unbidden from her eye

and fall across the crescent-shaped bruise decorating her cheek. She bandaged her finger and waited for the words that never came, waited for the heavy footfalls and callused hand upon her shoulder, body shaking in anticipation of the whispered criticism. She peered behind herself cautiously, then looked at the clock once more. There were still a few minutes left.

The thunder came again and Elsie dashed across the room to clean a spot of blood from the floor by the window, shuffling the curtain back into place so that no one could say it had been opened.

The oven timer dinged as a short flash of lightning illuminated Elsie's bluish neck, a purple necklace with golden jewels where the older bruises were fading. She looked at the clock as she placed the meal on the table: one plate, one set of cutlery, a candle, and the newspaper. The rain was hammering down on the roof and the door rattled on its hinges. The clock struck the evening hour behind her, the beginnings of the night, and Elsie trembled against the work-top, her wedding ring making soft clicking noises on the wood. A roar of thunder came together with a blinding flash of lightning and, as a silhouette across the curtains, she could see him stepping out of his car. The storm had arrived.

Rain-soaked
Redemption

Morgan DePue

Morgan DePue was born in Charlotte, NC, and raised in the small town of Lincolnton. A vagabond poet, she has no concrete location at present. Wasting no time pursuing her dreams, Morgan participates in several monthly readings and worked with the local Gaston College to establish monthly readings on campus. Previous and forthcoming publication credits include *Stepping Stones Magaine: ALMIA*, *Wild Goose Poetry Review*, *Main Street Rag* magazine, and *The BEST of the Main Street Rag Reading Series: Poetry Hickory 2011 Anthology*.

The rolling thunder beats the sky
black and blue
like the war drum
raging in my chest,
rumbling a song of warning,
every beat a malicious threat
meant to ward off those
who may heed the thunderstrike
without being thunderstruck.

The lightning is a strobe light
until the fury moves closer.
When her touch is visible,
see her fiery fingers
reaching into the Earth
like a child
molesting a cookie jar.
She always comes back empty-handed,
with each strike more furious
at her fruitless attempts
to find something in this world
worth holding on to
until, finally
she streaks across the sky
hoping the air
may hold the answers.

Jealous at the lightning's striking beauty,
which is only accentuated by her rage,
the wind blows the storm
like he's trying to rip
the tempest from the clouds.
Tree limbs wave in fear
and sacrifice their leaves
to Aeolian avarice.

As the storm rides in
on raging winds
the rain
makes her presence
known as a definite
with the permanence of pain.
Shooting droplets
like all the bullets
we have fired at our dreams,
knowing that nothing
leaves a sting
like failure,
especially when shortcomings
are measured in outcomes
not efforts.

The war drum thunder
beats the sky
until the earth quakes
in fear
and the lightning
keeps reaching
for the dreams
we buried in time capsules,
hidden in the Earth
unable to birth
their beauty.
The wind blows fury,
shooting rain like fire,
but the bluebirds
still fly,
singing songs of hope
and redemption
to the rain-soaked dreamers.

PRiDE and JOY

CAROLE BELLACERA

Carole Bellacera's work has appeared in magazines such as *Woman's World*, *The Star*, *Endless Vacation*, and *The Washington Post*. She is the author of four acclaimed novels published by Tor/Forge Books, and two other novels published by small presses.

Carole's first novel, *Border Crossings*, a hardcover published by Forge Books in May of 1999, was a 2000 RITA Award nominee for Best Romantic Suspense and Best First Book, and a nominee for the 2000 Virginia Literary Award in Fiction.

Other Books by Carole:
Spotlight (Forge Books, April 2000)
East of the Sun, West of the Moon (Forge Books, July 2001)
Understudy (Forge Books, June 2003)
Chocolate on a Stick (Baycrest Books, Sept 2005)
Tango's Edge (Beautiful Evening Books, Sept 2011)
Lily of the Springs (Beautiful Evening Books, March 2012)

VITTORIO STEPHARELLI STOOD AT THE WINDOW OF his apartment and watched his wife, Rose Maria, as she wearily climbed into their '93 Impala to head for her custodian job at a Days Inn in Palmdale. His eyes burned in an effort to hold back tears that had been held in for too many years. He rubbed a calloused hand over his worn cotton shirt, massaging the growing ache in his heart as the rattle-trap car backed out of the driveway and lumbered off down the palm-lined street. He hoped it would get her to the motel without breaking down again.

A hard March rain fell from a tarnished silver sky, promising several more inches by nightfall—more bad news for the unfortunate rich in the canyon, moaning in piteous horror as their three-million-dollar mansions collapsed under the ruthless crush of dense mud. But Vittorio had no sympathy for them. They were morons to keep rebuilding in such a treacherous place. Instead, he worried about Rose Maria in her cheap K-Mart flats and the half-price raincoat she'd picked up at the Salvation Army the first winter here in America. If the car broke down and she had to walk any distance, she would be soaked through.

After her taillights disappeared into the gloom, Vittorio shook his head and turned away from the window. It would all work out. God willing. Of course, that's what he'd believed when they'd left their small village in Sicily a decade ago, thinking that California would be the answer to all their problems.

But nothing had changed, even after he and Rose Maria and 18-year-old Chiara had become American citizens. They were barely getting by on his wife's income while Chiara went to public high school and worked an after-school job at McDonald's. Three years ago, Vittorio had been laid off by UPS, and while he drew unemployment pay, Rose Maria had started the job at Days Inn, leaving him to stay home to take care of Paolo.

Vittorio's gaze fell on the boy, and a familiar sadness settled upon him like the weight of the protective apron the X-ray technician had slipped on him two weeks ago during an exam. Not sadness for himself, but for Paolo.

The boy sat on the threadbare carpet, his dark head bent over a wooden pre-school puzzle. In his slender, artistic hand, Paolo held a wood piece shaped like a star. His lips pursed, he stared down at the puzzle for a long moment and then slowly fitted it into the correct place.

In the past, Vittorio had felt a lifting of his spirit at such an accomplishment of Paolo's—and something akin to hope—despite what all the doctors said. But that hadn't happened for years. Now, when he watched his only son painstakingly put one of those puzzles together, he felt only a sense of loss. And he wondered what might've been.

A sudden stench permeated the room, and with resignation, Vittorio looked at the boy. It was time for his diaper change. He trudged over to Paolo, bent down and slid his hands under the boy's arms.

"Come on, Paolo, let's get you changed, son." Using the strength of his upper body, Vittorio heaved Paolo to his feet, trying not to breathe in the ripe, pungent smell of fresh feces.

Paolo towered over him, four inches taller than Vittorio's 5'9". Liquid brown eyes stared vacantly as Vittorio maneuvered to his son's side, keeping one arm fastened around his shoulders as he guided him toward the bedroom. Paolo moved with slow, plodding steps as if somehow his body had a memory of this ritual. And who knew? Maybe it did.

Inside the bedroom he shared with his older sister, Paolo positioned himself on his back on the narrow twin bed and waited, his eyes fastened in boyish delight on a mobile of Sesame Street characters. Grinning up at them, he clapped his hands in delight.

Vittorio reached for the giant-sized tub of Wet Ones and grabbed an extra-large Depends from the box on the dresser, noting that there were only three left. *Should've bought more*, he thought. But he dismissed that thought with a shake of the head. It didn't matter.

Working with long-practiced efficiency, Vittorio pulled Paolo's sweatpants down past his knees and removed his diaper. The Depends people tried to make it easy by putting the diaper's fasteners on one side, allowing them to be put on standing up and without removing your clothes. But Paolo had been having it done this way since he was an infant, and change wasn't something he easily accepted.

Vittorio briskly cleaned Paolo up with several moistened wipes and slid a fresh diaper under the teenager's rump. His gaze focused on his son's flaccid, man-sized penis, and that's when the pain knifed through him—pain so intense it momentarily took his breath away.

His boy would never use that healthy-looking cock for anything other than pissing out of. He would never know the intense pleasure of making love to a beautiful woman…of impregnating a wife and feeling his heart swell with pride at the birth of a beautiful daughter or a strong, spirited son to carry on the family name.

Tears blurred Vittorio's vision as he fastened the diaper and tugged Paolo's sweatpants back up around his girlishly slender waist. The youth grinned up at the mobile and began to mutter gibberish, the only sounds he ever made—not Italian, not English… but some unknown language that made sense to no one but God.

Sixteen years ago in Italy, Vittorio had been the nervous young father of a two-year-old when Rose Maria went into labor with Paolo. The village midwife had arrived and ushered Vittorio out of the bedroom. Angelina, a neighbor from down the road and the local busybody, had seen the midwife rushing by with her medical bag. Within five minutes, she'd appeared at their door to take Chiara home with her until the baby was born. That's how it was in the old country. Neighbors—even busybodies—helped each other out without being asked. It was different here. They'd lived in the same apartment on Clair Del Avenue for ten years and still didn't know their neighbors' names. Of course, it was rare that any of them stayed longer than a few months.

Paolo had been silent when he came into the world on that sunny February afternoon. Vittorio hadn't even known he had a son until the midwife came out of the bedroom with bloody hands and a stone-like expression on her obese face and asked him to sit down.

The baby had been blue upon delivery, she told him, and Vittorio, naïve young man that he'd been, had taken her words literally, wondering how it was possible that an Italian couple could create a baby with blue skin. But the midwife had gone on to explain that Paolo had been born with the umbilical cord twisted around his neck, that he'd been without oxygen for an extended period of time, and though she'd managed to get him to breathe, it was likely there would be brain damage. With those words, life had changed for the whole family.

Vittorio straightened, took Paolo's hands in his, and gently pulled him to his feet. "Come, darling boy," he said in Italian. "It is time for 'Barney.' I will get your apple juice."

And then it will be nap-time for both of us.

Vittorio could almost believe Paolo understood him. The teen-ager gave a vacant grin and talked to himself as his father led him back into the living room and sat him down on the floor with his puzzles.

Vittorio turned on the TV and went into the kitchen to pour Paolo's juice. He hoped the government wouldn't cut off Rose Maria's food stamps. He'd done some research and had been reassured they wouldn't. But governments were known to lie, especially this one.

He'd thought America would be different. He'd believed California would be the answer. He'd swallowed it, Homer Simpson–style—the so-called American dream. D'ohhh! But the doctors here had failed them, too. Nothing they could do, they'd said. Paolo would always have the mentality of a toddler.

Vittorio gave Paolo his juice and watched as he greedily drank it down. The boy handed the glass back, his eyes glued to the TV where Barney flounced around, singing one of his dopey songs. Paolo loved it. He grinned at the TV in obvious delight and occasionally clapped his hands.

Vittorio sank onto the old tweed sofa—another relic from The Salvation Army—and with trembling fingers, lit a Camel. He took a long draw of it, then released the smoke in a flat, blue trail. His gaze fastened on the TV screen, but he wasn't really seeing it.

The phone call had come a week ago, late afternoon, long after Rose Maria had left for work. Vittorio had made the appointment for the following day. There had been no one to look after Paolo, so he'd taken the boy with him, riding the bus to Lakewood. In his accented English, he'd explained the situation to the pretty lady behind the glass window. She'd glanced into the waiting room where Paolo sat scribbling on a coloring book, and nodded. And while his boy made meaningless marks on a wall-climbing Spiderman, Vittorio listened to an Indian doctor, ten years his junior, tell him he was going to die.

No one is ever prepared for news like that, and that afternoon, he'd been no exception. Lung cancer, the young doctor sadly informed him. Vittorio had searched his mind for the correct English words; even after ten years, he still thought in Italian.

"How long?" he finally blurted.

A shrug and a downward cast of the doctor's dark, foreign eyes. "Six to eight months…maybe less."

In a state of shock, Vittorio ushered Paolo out of the waiting room and headed for the bus stop. As they made their way back home, one continuous thought ran through his head.

I cannot do this to Rose Maria. She has been through enough.

What kind of God would burden a beautiful young woman with a mentally disabled child, force her to work her fingers to the bone cleaning toilets and scrubbing floors to bring home a meager paycheck, and every day, growing older before his eyes? Only 40, she looked 55, her once lustrous black hair streaked with gray, her legs deformed by a railroad map of varicose veins. And now, she'd have to watch her husband die a slow, torturous death from cancer, leaving her with a bright, attractive teenage daughter who dreamed of going to college and a helpless toddler trapped in the body of a teenage boy.

No. It would not do. All his life, Vittorio had lived by God's terms. It was time now to die by his own.

By the time "Barney" was over, Paolo's lids were starting to droop. Vittorio's heart jolted as he realized how late it was. He got to his feet, waited a moment for the dizziness to pass, and then went to his son.

"Come on, my boy. Nap-time."

Paolo didn't protest as Vittorio hauled him to his feet. He never did when it came to bed-time. Vittorio wondered if it was because in his dreams, Paolo was a normal boy, playing soccer, kissing girls, doing homework, sneaking smokes, and drinking beer. Leading a normal life. Vittorio wanted to believe that.

In the bedroom, he changed Paolo's diaper and covered him with his grandmother's hand-embroidered quilt that had accompanied them from Italy. Through the small window looking out on a wet parking lot, Vittorio watched the rain fall. The numbers on the digital alarm clock on the bedside stand glowed red—3:30. It was so dark in the room that it seemed closer to nightfall. For a moment, Vittorio peered down at his son. His eyes were already closed, his long lashes curling upwards like a girl's. Vittorio felt as if someone had reached a hand inside his chest and manually squeezed his heart, sending a reverberating ache down through the soles of his feet. Turning away, he stiffened, his gaze fastening upon a framed picture on the nightstand. He'd seen it a million times before, of course, but he couldn't stop himself from picking it up.

Paolo, at two years old, stared back at him, his dark hair tousled, brown eyes wide-spaced and luminous. The frame was blue porcelain painted with the words "Pride and Joy." A stranger looking at the photo wouldn't have seen anything unusual about the boy. Only his parents saw the blankness in his eyes, and knew that their "pride and joy" would forever be two years old, even as his body grew.

And yet...it was true. Paolo was their pride and joy. He'd been cherished from the very beginning, cherished now. By all of them—Rose Maria, Chiara, and yes, by Vittorio. But he couldn't, he *wouldn't* leave Rose Maria the burden of caring for him alone. In a year, Chiara would be off to college. She'd already been accepted by Southern Cal on a full scholarship. Her dream was to be a doctor and work in the mental health field. There was only one way now for that dream to come true.

Vittorio would wait until he was sure Paolo was asleep. With a soft sigh, the boy turned toward the wall, clutching a stuffed beagle to his chest. His breathing grew deep and even. Vittorio wanted to believe—he had to believe—that even now, Paolo was lost in a dream where he could do all the things he'd never do in this lifetime. And soon...God willing, that dream would be a reality.

Together, Vittorio would make the journey with his son, and they would talk to each other as they never had before—man to man. And Paolo would thank him for releasing him; he would understand that it was the only answer—the only way to save Rose Maria and Chiara from a life of drudgery.

Vittorio brushed a lock of black hair away from Paolo's forehead and gazed down at him through blurred eyes. The boy didn't stir.

It was time.

He glanced at the clock. It was just after 4:00 pm. Rose Maria wouldn't get off work until 11:00, and with the rain still coming down as it was predicted to do throughout the night, it would probably take her at least a half an hour to get home. That left seven and a half hours. Plenty of time.

He walked into the kitchen and pulled open the utensil drawer, staring down at its contents. That's when he heard the voice of his conscience. *What if you're wrong? What if, by doing this deed, even if it is to give your beloved wife her freedom, you condemn yourself to eternal hell?*

His Catholic upbringing still held a powerful sway over him. Rarely did they ever miss Sunday Mass. He went to confession on a regular basis, and recited the Stations of the Cross with Rose Maria every Easter. And yet...here he was, getting ready to commit two of the deadliest of sins.

He reached into the utensil tray and took out a paring knife, running his thumb along the blade to make sure it was sharp enough. A thin line of blood welled from the cut. He wiped his thumb on a dishtowel and turned toward the door. He'd read somewhere that bleeding to death was a peaceful way to go—and unlike pills, it would be reliable.

Before his prognosis, it would never have entered his mind to do such a thing. But once he'd realized he had only months to live, and Rose Maria would be left to carry the burden alone, Vittorio had felt as if God had broken a contract with him. All his life, he'd been a good man. He'd worked hard for his family and cared for Paolo with loving hands. Never had he ever been bitter about the trials thrust upon him. He'd taken each one like a man, a strong man who believed that God dealt out hardships to make him a *better* man. And yet, even now, God was still dealing out the blows.

This time, it was too much. Not for him. He had the easy part. What could be easier than dying? Anyway, he truly believed that death was only a journey into a better place. And despite all the teachings, he just couldn't believe that he would go to Hell for this, for rescuing his family. But even if he did, then it was a price he was willing to pay so that Rose Maria and Chiara—and Paolo—would have a better life.

Clutching the dishtowel in one hand, the knife in the other, he stepped into Paolo's room. The boy still slept, but now he was on his back, breathing slowly and deeply. It was a sign, Vittorio realized. And just like that, all his doubts disappeared into the ether.

Paolo was giving him permission to do what he had to do. For a moment, Vittorio stared down at his only son, and this time he allowed the tears to brim over and slide down his cheeks. Finally he moved, placing the dishtowel beneath Paolo's chin and tucking its ends under his shoulders. It wouldn't do to have Rose Maria be forced to clean up such a mess. He reached out and brushed Paolo's hair back from his forehead.

"*L'amo, il ragazzo di darling,*" he whispered. *I love you, darling boy.*

Flattening his palm on the top of Paolo's head, Vittorio poised the tip of the knife at the left side of his throat, under his ear. Just as he started to thrust the blade into his skin, Paolo's eyes opened. It wasn't an accusing look or one of fear. Just the usual blank stare of an unconscious mind.

Still, Vittorio felt the need to reassure him. "Shhhh," he whispered. "*Ritornare dormire, il ragazzo di angelo. Quando lei si sveglia, sarà tutto migliore.*" *Go back to sleep, angel boy. When you wake, it will be all better.*

His hand slid down Paolo's face to gently cover his eyes. With his other hand, he thrust the blade into the tender skin of his son's throat.

↩

Black spots danced in front of Vittorio's eyes. He had no feeling below the knees; his arms felt like concrete. Yet, he still registered the cold of the porcelain bathtub against his naked skin and the slickness of his blood in which he lay.

It was taking a long time to die. With the same knife he'd used on Paolo, he'd cut deeply into both wrists, allowing the lifeblood to drain from his cancer-ridden body.

He wasn't sure how much time had passed. His thoughts had eddied and flowed, taking him back to his boyhood in Catania, revisiting some of his happiest days. Like the one when he'd first laid eyes on Rose Maria as she stood on an arched stone bridge gazing down at the turtles in the stream. Her black hair had glistened with blue highlights under the summer sun. And when she'd turned and smiled, he'd felt as if he'd been struck by lightning.

And later, their wedding day in the village. Rose Maria's hand had trembled as he'd slipped the plain gold band onto her finger. Other wonderful days and beautiful memories...his hand touching the lovely mound of her belly as their first-born kicked in her womb...the glorious day Chiara burst into the world, full of fire and robust health...the first tender moments cradling his son, knowing he would never be "normal," but finding it nearly impossible to believe that as he looked into the baby's perfect little face.

Lost in the memories, it took a moment before he realized he'd heard a sound that he shouldn't be hearing—a key rattling in the lock, and then the opening of the door. He blinked sleepily and tried to sit up. But his muscles refused to work.

"Vitto? *Il mio amore*, I'm home," Rose Maria called out. "They sent us home because of flooding on the ground floor."

Alarm flickered deep inside Vittorio, but it seemed as if his brain was the only thing left working in his body. *No*, he gave a silent shriek. *This is not the way it is supposed to happen. I do not want to know. I do not want to hear!*

But he could hear clearly. Her footsteps coming down the hallway.

"Why is it so quiet in here? And why are the lights off, Vitto? It is too early for bed."

She would check on Paolo first. She always did. Vittorio squeezed his eyes shut; he wished he had the strength to move his hands so he could cover his ears.

For a moment, there was nothing but silence. And then, Rose Maria began to scream. Vittorio knew it was a sound he would hear throughout eternity.

⌐

Chiara Stepharelli methodically tore the acceptance letter from Southern Cal into tiny pieces and watched as they floated down into the wastebasket. Her eyes were dry, her hands steady. All the tears had already been cried. She had no more. She'd finally come to terms with her destiny. After all, some dreams were never meant to be.

She turned to the mirror and swept a hand down her crisp, pink blouse embroidered with "Merry Maids." It was her day to work while Mama stayed home with Paolo. Tomorrow it would be her turn to stay at home. Chiara pulled her long, dark hair back into a ponytail, and left the room.

She stopped at the threshold of Paolo's room—the one she used to share with him before what the police called "the incident." Mama had moved in there, giving Chiara the master bedroom, saying, "A girl your age needs her own room."

Mama had just finished changing Paolo's diaper. She looked up at Chiara, lavender smudges of fatigue under her dark eyes. "You leaving for work now?"

Chiara nodded. "You need me to pick up anything at the store on the way home?"

Her mother shook her graying head. "We're out of food stamps. We'll have to make do until next month." She pulled up Paolo's sweatpants and gave him a gentle smack on his thigh.

Paolo scrambled up into a sitting position and grinned with delight when he saw his sister. The healed scar along his throat stood out starkly against his pale skin. Chiara stepped into the room and went over to give her brother a hug.

"Will you stop and see Papa after work?" her mother asked.

"Of course," said Chiara. "How was he last night?"

Mama shook her head, her dark eyes glimmering with sadness. "Not good. He did not recognize me. The doctor says his time is growing short."

Chiara couldn't look at her mother. Instead, she kept her eyes on Paolo's innocently happy face. "It would've been better if he'd just died that day. How can you *do it*, Mama?" She finally forced herself to meet her mother's gaze. "Feed him, change his diaper, stay with him until he falls asleep? After what he did to our helpless Paolo? Please tell me…how can you still love Papa?"

Rose Maria didn't speak for a long moment. She simply put her hand on Chiara's shoulder and gazed at her son. "Simply because I do." She paused a moment, then added, "Do not hate him, Chiara. He did what he thought would be best for us. He did it because he loved us."

Chiara digested her mother's words, trying to force back the bile rising in her throat. Finally, when she managed to rein in her emotions, she turned to her mother and said quietly, "And that is what makes it so appalling. He did it out of love."

She turned and walked quickly out of the room. A few minutes later, she waited for the bus that would take her to Merry Maids. It pulled up in front of her, and she boarded, taking a seat in the back. Her eyes fastened on one of the ads on the panel running along the length of the bus. It showed a young man in a graduation gown holding a diploma and wearing a happy grin. In huge block letters, the caption read, "It's All About Education!"

Chiara stared at it a moment, and then pulled an *Entertainment Weekly* magazine from her bag and began to read about the latest Kardashian scandal.

sowing the wind

ALAN PHILPS

Alan left the UK in 1974 with a degree in Material Science to go and work as a plant engineer on the copper mines in Zambia, Africa. Several years in Zambia, followed by ten years in South Africa, left him with a wanderlust for exploring wild places. When he returned to England to work as a Quality Manager in the construction and chemical industries, he carried that fascination with him. Having waded through the aftermath of terrorist explosions, faced bayonet-wielding soldiers, and collected the bodies of birds who mistook pools of arsenic for water, he found the peace of the English countryside stifling. To counteract the boredom he started writing, creating worlds filled with savagery and darkness—worlds fit for heroes to conquer. In addition to a number of short stories he has completed a three-book fantasy series called *The Black Tide*, where a primitive world is invaded by creatures that feed on human flesh.

"OH…GOOD SHOT."

John watched his opponent's ball arc across the cloudless sky and drop onto the green, six feet from the pin. "With luck you'll get down in one from there," he said, trying to be gracious.

"Luck," Matt growled as he threw the club into his bag. "You're the one with all the luck—two eagles, two birdies, and no bogeys. I always said you were born with a silver spoon in your mouth, or is it a golden club in your hand these days?"

John tried hard not to grin but Matt was right, he was playing an amazing round of golf. He had better keep his delight hidden however. Matt could be a poor loser. "You won four hundred off me the other night at the dog race. Doesn't that count?" he tried.

"Four hundred? If we split the last hole, I'll still owe you eight. I think those lessons with your Club Pro have been a waste of time. I've a good mind to make him pay!"

Matt grumbled all the way up the last fairway, then three-putted into the hole.

"I'll tell you what," John offered as they approached the clubhouse, worried that Matt would make a scene. "It's our anniversary tomorrow night. Why don't you pick up the tab for the best seats at the *Merchant of Venice* and a meal for two at Dino's and we'll call it quits?"

He could see Matt mentally counting the cost before coming to a decision.

"Sure," he agreed with a smile. "I'd do anything to make sure you and Pauline have a special night tomorrow."

John knew the evening wouldn't cost more than three hundred dollars, but kept quiet, happy to play Matt's game. After all, he and Matt had been friends since high school. "You can afford it," he insisted, trying to improve Matt's mood. "Tell me again how much you got for your dad's sawmill."

"Eight million," Matt replied with a smug grin.

"Not bad for a penniless punk from the woods," he claimed as they walked into the ranch-style clubhouse of California's Torrey Pines.

John ordered the drinks and was content to let Matt tell him once more how he became a self-made millionaire.

"After you left high school to study law at Berkley, I went to work for my old man. I thought he was going to teach me the ropes, train me to take over the mill, but it wasn't like that. To him I was just another employee earning his keep brushing the floors and keeping the equipment running. I spent ten years covered in wood dust and engine oil. I learned a lot about machines during that time and how to keep them running. Since I was paid the same pittance as everyone else, it was just as well I could keep my old Mustang going on nothing more than spit and air. I couldn't believe it when old man Harrison came 'round one day and offered Dad half a million dollars for the place. Heck! That was a lot more than it was worth."

Like a professional story-teller, Matt kept his audience waiting by swallowing most of his drink before continuing his tale.

"The old fool turned him down, but it got me wondering. I found out there was a new highway going right through our stockyard. Harrison was on the local planning board and must have thought he'd buy the place and make a fortune selling it on to the developers. He even tried to get the route changed after Dad refused him but he was as old as Methuselah and died before the final approvals came through. It just goes to show you can fight all you want for more but you still can't take it with you."

As Matt grimaced at the vagaries of fate, John finished his beer and gestured at the barman for a refill. It had been hot out there.

"Why wouldn't your dad sell the place?" John asked, even though he knew the answer.

"He said the mill had been in his family for over sixty years and he'd worked in it man and boy. He'd never sell it," Matt told him. "One day he got up early to have a look around the mill, however, and left me making breakfast. When he didn't come back, I went looking for him. Some of the men found him lying dead next to one of the pulleys. The sheriff said the bolts had rusted through and it was just his bad luck that he was standing beneath it when it fell."

Matt became silent, staring off into the distance.

"Everyone liked Dad," he said eventually. He added with a heavy sigh, "Folks came from miles around to pay their respects. It just don't seem right that his bad luck should be the start of *my* good fortune. It just don't seem right."

"The king is dead, long live the king," John reminded him and was rewarded with a strained smile.

"Your dad didn't have to die for you to come into money," Matt pointed out, his eyes turning agate hard. "How much was that trust fund worth?"

"Enough," was all John was prepared to say of a figure that would keep him comfortable for the rest of his days. "After all, money isn't everything."

"Funny how those with money always say stupid things like that," Matt claimed with a thinly veiled sneer. "Anyway," he added, sensing that he had overstepped his bounds, "here's to you and Pauline, may your life together be long and happy." He raised his glass and smiled over the rim, a smile that reminded John of younger, football-filled days.

"To Pauline," he agreed, raising his glass in reply.

"So that's my story," Matt said as he settled back in the leather chair. "Now tell me what you've been doing for the last ten years and why you're working when your father owns half of Long Beach? I thought that law degree of yours would have gotten you a nice seat on one of Daddy's boards of directors?"

John smothered his irritation at the sarcasm. They had been best friends in high school, but even then money—or the lack of it—had been a thorn in Matt's side.

"Three years of law showed me that I'd sooner jump off a cliff than do that for the rest of my life."

"So what do you do for Piggot and Sons?"

"We're claims adjusters. We investigate insurance claims. Most of the major insurance companies use our services before handing over the big money. I specialize in personal possessions such as artwork and jewelry. You'd be amazed how many women suddenly lose a diamond earring or two when times get tough."

Matt snorted. "So you like brow-beating middle-aged women?"

John felt his cheeks burning. "I like reading the signs. The Porsche mothballed in the garage, water rings on the coffee table, last month's manicure, leaves in the pool, that sort of thing. They're all signs that money is tight and luxuries like the pool boy and live-in maid have been put aside. I like pitting my wits against people who think they can lie to me and get away with it."

Matt started to smile. It began small then grew and grew, until his cheeks were plump red apples and his eyes wrinkled prunes. He put a hand across his mouth to hide his amusement. "Then those middle-aged Elaines had better watch out," he chuckled. "Ol' John is on to them."

"I've got to go," John told him, deciding he'd had enough for one day. "I need to pick up Pauline's anniversary present from the jewelers before they close."

"Lucky Pauline," Matt said. His lips curved to make a smile but his eyes glinted like pieces of ice.

$\backsim$

"I suppose you'll be playing golf with Matt again on Friday?" Pauline said as she put on her earrings and studied her reflection in the huge mirror of the en suite bathroom.

"Only if you don't mind, sweetheart," John replied kissing her forehead, being careful not to disturb the deliberately tousled blond hair.

"You've never spoken of him before, but he turns up out of the blue one day and suddenly he's your new best friend," she claimed, blinking to hide her disappointment. "In the two months he's been here you've spent more time with him than you have with me."

"I know. It's just that I feel sorry for him. He'd come to school as a kid covered in bruises. He loved his dad, even though he beat him most days. What he hated most in the world was being poor. I went away to college and left him behind without a thought. He was a bright kid with good grades but he couldn't get out of there. He didn't have my trust fund. Instead he worked long hours at his dad's sawmill. Now he's got money and wants to brag about it and throw it around. I can't turn my nose up at him. I owe him that much at least."

"But…"

"Look, sweetheart, I've told him things have to change, that I need to spend more time with you. He understands. I've booked a cabin in the mountains for next week. We'll walk and fish and enjoy being alone together. It will be like a second honeymoon."

Pauline made a small, wry smile before laying a warm hand on his arm. "Careful, tiger," she warned him. "On our first honeymoon you pulled a very important muscle."

"It was all that jogging," he insisted, putting on his tie.

"Of course it was, dear," she replied, pouting and applying lipstick. "But this time we'll take things a little more slowly around the block. Okay?"

When John gave her a firm tap on the derriere, she chuckled.

⇆

They never made it to the cabin.

⇆

John poured coffee into two mugs, adding milk to both and two spoons of sugar to one.

"This one is for Matt," he said stirring the coffee with the sugar. "You know all that sugar rots your teeth," he whispered. As he tipped half the contents down the drain he added, "Not that you'll be worrying much about teeth after today."

Leaving the mugs behind he strolled down the corridor to the bathroom. He took a pair of latex gloves from his pocket and put them on. He didn't want to leave fingerprints here. Opening the bathroom cabinet, he located a bottle labeled Lunestra. They were Matt's sleeping pills. Back in the kitchen he dropped two tablets into his mug of coffee and left the open bottle next to the coffee machine.

Taking both mugs he went into the living room and put them on the coffee table. He stood upright and glared at the body sprawled across the marble floor.

"Don't bother to get up," he muttered, seeing the bruise on the side of Matt's forehead coloring up nicely.

"What you forgot, you bastard," he hissed at the man on the floor, "is that claims adjusters wade through bullshit every day to get at the truth, and you," he punctuated his point with a savage kick to the ribs, "are a crock of shit!"

He warned himself about getting side-tracked. He had to stick to the plan. He had busted a few award-winning scams in his time, so he knew a good plan when he saw it. He had used everything he knew about Matt and wrapped it into a neat little package, one that would pay him back for what he'd done. Sitting down on the white leather settee, he stared at the coffee and reminded himself why he was there.

‿

Pauline had never liked Matt. At the time, John had put it down to the weekends at the golf course, the football games, the betting at the racetrack. It was like the old days in high school when they would bet on everything. Sometimes Matt won, sometimes he did. Only this time they were older and had more money. When Pauline complained, he did what any other caring husband would have done. He arranged for them to spend more time together.

When he told Matt that things could not continue as they had, Matt sulked. His temper hadn't improved after another appalling round of early-morning golf. It was late that Friday afternoon when John got a call at work to say that Pauline had been in an accident and had been taken to County General. He sped across town like a maniac, his hands shaking, his voice hoarse from praying she'd be all right, but he got to her side too late. She died on the gurney before he could get there.

In the shell-shocked weeks that followed, Matt was his caring, constant companion. He looked after him, reminded him when to eat and shave. He helped arrange the funeral, chose the floral tributes, and even picked Pauline's parents up from the airport. Matt couldn't have been a better friend. Two weeks after the funeral John dragged himself back to work and Matt returned home. The guys at the office gave him the time and space he needed to come to terms with his loss. Matt insisted they go out and John tagged along, not seeing the point.

It was two months before he could bring himself to open her closet and bundle her clothes into plastic bags for the charity shop. Everything was thrown in. The pink pumps for lunch with friends, the green jacket worn to the movies. He bundled memories so sharp they cut like knives into six black bags and tossed them into the back of the car like garbage.

It was while he was sorting through the personal items taken from her car that he came across her diary and phone. He sat down with three fingers of Jack Daniels, needing its fiery courage flooding through his veins before letting her words touch him from beyond the grave. He opened the diary and turned to the days immediately before the crash. As he flipped through the pages he noticed the name "Matt" several times.

Matt came early…Matt is always here…Matt was horrible to me, said I wasn't good enough…Matt scares me. I wish he'd go away…I wish John would send Matt away.

As he closed the diary, a vagrant tear fell to his cheek. Poor Pauline, why hadn't she told him how she felt? When he checked her text messages, he saw *why* she hadn't spoken to him.

Bitch. I've had enough of your whining. Once more and I'm gonna tell him about your uncle and what you two got up to when you were a kid.

That message had come from Matt. John was stunned by its nastiness. What the hell was going on? A quick flick through her other messages threw up several more from Matt, all in the same vicious, threatening tone. It was the last message, however, that chilled his blood.

Too late bitch, you were warned.

That one was dated the day of the crash.

For hours he sat in stunned silence, thinking about what he'd learned. The police had checked the car after the accident and said it hadn't been tampered with, but Matt was a fiend with cars. After a couple of hours, armed with paper and a pen, John drew up a plan.

Two days later he'd put that plan into action. Sitting on the settee, he could see its result. Early that evening he'd turned up at Matt's door with his ankle bandaged, walking with the aid of a heavy cane. Matt had been sympathetic about the fictitious fall. When he bent down to lift John's injured foot onto a stool, he had been in the right position but totally unprepared for the blow to the head.

"Now for the grave," John announced, his voice a discordant echo played against the subdued sounds coming from the road outside.

Striding through the kitchen he deliberately avoided looking at the knives. He opened the garage door and descended the steep concrete steps beyond. Taking Matt's yellow golf cap from its hook, he pulled it down over his ears. He grabbed a shovel from the cluster of tools in the corner and opened the door to the back-yard. It closed behind him with a bang as he walked out onto the grass with his shoulders hunched. He and Matt were of a similar build. He wanted witnesses to swear they had seen Matt in the garden.

Luckily the light from the house provided enough illumination for the task he had in mind. With a muted curse he heeled the shovel into the newly-planted flower bed. Loamy soil and uprooted begonias soon lay in a long line on the grass, leaving a shallow depression in the flower bed six feet long by three feet wide. Before returning to the house he scuffed his shoes on the grass to clean them. Back in the garage he left the shovel propped up just inside the door with dirt clinging to its face and the yellow cap hanging from the handle.

In the living room, he knelt down and rubbed dirt into Matt's hands before seizing him by the wrists and dragging him across the kitchen to the garage door. Keeping the door open with his foot, he grabbed him under the arms and pulled him up. It took every ounce of strength he had to get Matt upright and leaning against his hip. With a twist of his shoulders, John threw him into the garage. There were a number of satisfying clunks as Matt rolled down the concrete steps and ended up in a huddle of arms and legs at the bottom.

John found he was breathing hard as he switched off the garage light. In the powder room he tore off the gloves, wrapped them in toilet paper, then flushed them down the toilet. He returned to the settee and sat down. Looking around, he found himself agreeing with Pauline's initial assessment. Matt's house, although rented, was bigger than theirs, his car newer, his lawn greener, his furniture more contemporary. There was one area where Matt couldn't compete, however. Pauline had been John's pride and joy, his brightest jewel. At school Matt had tried charming John's girlfriends. Most of them dismissed him as a creep, with him condemning them as gold-diggers in return. If he had tried that nonsense with Pauline…?

Picking up the cold coffee, he held it to his lips knowing that drinking it would push him past the point of no return. Afterwards he'd have ten minutes before he fell asleep. The knives in the kitchen called to him. They promised blood, they promised justice, they promised an eye for an eye. Taking a deep breath, he drank his coffee. The problem was, he wasn't certain. In his guts, he felt sure Matt had killed Pauline, like he also felt sure Matt had killed his own father and that old man, Harrison. The signs were all there, but he wasn't certain. No one could cut a man's throat based on a gut feeling—at least, he couldn't. He had to stick to the plan.

Leaving a swallow in the bottom of the cup, he checked the time. He waited for ten minutes then picked up the phone. Trembling hands dialed 911.

"Can I speak to the police?" Already he was feeling the drug's effects: a tightness across the forehead, a dryness at the back of the throat, the compulsion to sleep. "Hurry up," he whispered knowing he didn't have much time left.

"This is the dispatcher, how can I help?" a female voice crackled in his ear.

"Please," he croaked, his vision swimming. "I've been…drugged. I'm at…16 Pensacola Avenue. Please…hurry. He's coming back."

At last he let the phone slip from his grasp and lay back with a sigh. It was done. Now he could rest. The police would be here soon.

They would find him unconscious on the settee with Matt equally unconscious in the garage. They would find the dirt on Matt's hands and a shallow grave in his garden. It would look like a murder gone wrong, that Matt slipped down the steps before he could finish his grisly work. It would be enough for them to look at Pauline's death with fresh eyes and see Matt as a potential killer. They would dig until they found the truth. Then John would know.

Lying back, he closed his eyes and relaxed, waiting for the sirens. It was the click of a door that brought him back to life. He stared in disbelief as Matt staggered into the kitchen with the shovel in his hand. His hair was disheveled, his left eye bloodshot. An arm was pressed close to his body as if cradling a broken rib.

"What the hell happened?" he demanded as he staggered towards John.

"Oh shit," John whispered. Unable to fight it any longer, his eyes closed and he tumbled head over heels into the darkness.

⌒

John awoke with a start to find himself in a hospital bed. A quick check confirmed he still had all his appendages. As he lay there waiting for the police and their questions, all he could think about was Matt. What happened? Where was he?

"Did you find the man who did this to me?" he asked the young police officer when he turned up an hour or so later.

"No, sir," the man replied with a nervous smile, ready to make copious notes with a tiny pencil. "We found you alone and unconscious. The ambulance arrived soon after we did and brought you here. Who did you say drugged you?"

With a sinking heart John gave them Matt's description.

The next morning, discharged from the hospital with the doctor's blessing and a bill as long as his arm, John opened his front door and stepped into a silent house. A piece of paper on the hall table caught his eye. The hand writing looked oddly familiar. He picked it up and read it.

I didn't see that coming—still, no hard feelings. For the record, I fixed that bitch just like I fixed my dad. We're better off without them.

Now there is just the two of us, like before. Since we're having such fun, here are the rules—there are no rules. Catch me if you can, John—but not before I catch you first!

As he read Matt's words, something hardened inside. Now that he was certain, the analytical part of his mind took control. Picking up a pen, he started listing the ingredients for a new plan.

Change the locks
Organize a leave of absence
Find Matt—Follow the money
Raid the trust fund
Buy a sniper rifle and bullets!

Matt thought this was all a game but he was very wrong. For John, the stakes were suddenly much higher. His friend had made a fatal mistake in assuming that John was the same boy he'd known in high school. He didn't know about the army and the marksmanship training. Matt had sown the wind; now he would reap the whirlwind.

"Run, Matt," John whispered. "Run as fast as you can, old friend. There's a storm coming!"

PROVISIONAL BLISS

HERB SHALLCROSS

Herb Shallcross was born and raised in Philadelphia, where he graduated from Drexel University with a BS in Psychology and a certificate in writing and publishing in 2007. He now lives in Queens with his amazing doctor wife. His poetry has appeared or will soon appear online at *Four and Twenty Poetry* and *APIARY Magazine*, and has been anthologized in *In the Garden of the Crow* from Elektrik Milk Bath Press.

I was born into sunshine
But never could stop eyeing
The thunderheads conspiring
On the horizon.

My mother would die,
Father would die, I
Would be left to fend for myself
Scrawny and powerless
Against the lashings of the wind and rain.
Floodwater would churn around my ankles
And climb toward my knees
In absolute darkness, except
When lightning would illuminate
The horror in all directions:
My loneliness.

This impending storm
Has shaped my every choice,
Tempered my every emotion.
I'm still fretting that damned storm;
I like to think I've made provisions.

the Letter

LARRY LEFKOWITZ

The stories, poetry, and humor of Larry Lefkowitz have appeared in many publications in the US, Israel, and the UK. Lefkowitz is looking for a publisher for his novel *Lieberman*. The plot of the novel concerns a literary critic, the assistant to the literary critic, and the wife of the critic. Very literary and filled with humor. Excerpts and chapters have been published in print and online.

MARIE. PAUL'S FIRST LOVE. HOW OFTEN HAD ALICE
thought of that name? Now, fingering the few gray strands among
the brown in the mirror, she could not help wondering: was Marie
really so much prettier? At least Marie was blessedly free of her own
tendency to squint, which Paul had teased her about affectionately
in the days of their "courtship." Alice had accepted Paul's valuation
of it as "cute." At twenty-five it may have been, but now…defiantly
Alice squinted at herself in the mirror. Sticking out her tongue was
to ask too much of her capabilities of self-parody.

Paul and Marie hadn't worked out, to Paul's regret. Paul, honest
in all things, freely admitted it, though always he added, "It was for
the best. Marie was too much for me." Sometimes he elaborated.
"Too demanding. She wanted somebody with more money."

Alice pictured Marie as vivacious, well coiffured, a carefully
positioned wave of hair slanting down chicly over her forehead, a
heavy bracelet of rhinestones encircling her tanned arm. It was,
fortunately, a mental picture; Paul did not keep an actual picture
of Marie—to have to compete with that permanent youthfulness
would have been a very uneven contest. Alice imagined Paul as having been but a trifle of Marie's, something she brought out of her
jewelry box when she was in need of someone to escort her to the
theater (Paul said they liked to attend the theater) while she looked
for richer game in the audience. Alice thought of her as using a lor-
gnette for this purpose, like some woman in a Henry James story.

After Alice and Paul married, Marie wrote with decreasing frequency to him, her bold script exactly the handwriting that Alice
pictured her as possessing. The perfume of the envelope was equally
suitable—strong, no-nonsense, bespeaking a woman who knew
exactly what she wanted and who was prepared to wait until she got
it. She had written one *de rigueur* letter to Alice after their marriage.
Part of it she remembered: "I hope you will be happy with Paul—
he's a dear. He has many precious qualities." Its patronizing manner was disturbing, as she was certain clever Marie had intended.
It caused Alice to regard Marie with hostility instead of the vague
dislike natural toward a former love of one's husband and which
a letter of sincere good wishes could have turned to appreciation.

Occasionally a letter arrived addressed to Paul in the bold script. In Alice's imagination each time the script seemed to have grown bolder. He would remark to Alice, "Poor Marie, each time a new 'beau,' each wealthier than the last. She hints that she is all but married to the latest one—and her next letter hints the same with regard to somebody else."

"She must be having a difficult time of it," Alice replied when Paul made this familiar observation after reading Marie's latest letter. Alice was not sure whether she really believed Marie was having a difficult time of it or whether she simply wished to convince Paul that Marie was incapable of settling down.

"Marie was always a bit fickle," Paul said. Alice strained to decipher if this observation contained a hint of regret, but she could not decide.

"With all those wealthy men to choose from, I would be fickle, too," she said lightly. Immediately she regretted her utterance. Paul looked down at the table, drummed on it lightly with his fingers and said, after a long moment, "Maybe you're right."

Alice knew that Paul was wondering whether if he had had more money then—even the amount that he presently possessed which, while hardly wealthy by what appeared to be Marie's standards, was considerably more than he had had when pursuing her—if *he* wouldn't have prevented her fickleness. Alice wondered often if Paul now regretted being married to her. If, with his present improved circumstances, he could marry Marie except for the fact that he was married to her. She was tempted to ask him yet feared—not his denial, which would be forthcoming, but his tone in saying it which might reveal something else. If she discovered a hint of regret, coming upon the deepening delta of wrinkles at the corners of her eyes and her increasing squint, it would have amounted to an admission.

Once when Paul said, after reading a letter from Marie, "I wonder if she looks the same," Alice had suggested, without considering the possible consequences, that he invite her to visit and find out. Paul had looked worried and said, "No, Marie leads too exciting a life. She would find us dull." He had laughed, making a joke of it. Alice suspected that he feared Marie would truly find them dull and poke fun gently in that not-so-gentle way of hers. Alice was relieved he had rejected her suggestion to invite Marie; she had realized immediately that it was a mistake—if dazzling Marie appeared on the scene, anything-but-dazzling Alice wouldn't have a chance. Maybe Paul realized it, too.

Thereafter, whenever the perfumed letters arrived, Alice feared that Marie would invite herself. If she ever had, Paul had not yet passed on the invitation. Alice sometimes believed Marie *did* invite herself and that Paul refused to allow it, feared it, and so did not tell her.

Alice never saw Marie's letters after they arrived. Paul either threw them away or kept them in a safe place. Alice couldn't prevent herself keeping an eye out for them in his bureau drawers when she placed clean shirts or socks inside; she was relieved when she never found them. Such keepsakes were the last thing that she needed.

At the next arrival of the "perfumed hand," as she gothically described to herself Marie's letters, Alice happened to be in a good mood, perhaps caused by a day that had been unusually pleasant in many small ways; especially she had enjoyed walking on the colored leaves which gathered on the sidewalk, squishing them crisply, a joy she did not consciously associate with Marie's letter which had arrived a short time before. And so, as Paul finished reading the letter, she ventured a joke, "Which Rockefeller *this* time?"

"She's tired of Rockefellers," Paul said in a serious tone.

"Oh? Ready to settle for something simpler?"

"So it seems."

"Had enough of drinking from the golden bowl, has she?" Alice persisted, her good mood overriding the voice within her that urged, "Caution, caution."

"Yes, now she would settle for one of copper," he said slowly.

"Well, it's not too late. Surely she can find *someone*." Alice regretted where the conversation was leading, yet felt helpless to stop it. She was curious and fearful at this new turn.

"I dare say she can," he said evenly.

Enough had been said, Alice decided. She hoped that Paul would tear up the letter, or at least throw it in the garbage. She would have given anything for that, to be rid of the letter whose presence was threatening. Paul, however, carefully replaced the letter in its perfumed envelope (which seemed to Alice stronger than ever) and put it in his jacket pocket. He then turned the conversation to other matters and it was only with difficulty during dinner that Alice kept her eyes from the pocket of his jacket.

She dreaded the next letter from Marie. Her anxiety was not helped by Paul's asking much too casually a week later, "Any mail?"

"Just the usual. Expecting something special?" She tried to sound casual, as well.

He hesitated. "I thought maybe Marie would drop a line."

"I see," she said.

"Now, Alice, there is no need to use that tone of voice. I have explained that once I loved Marie. But that was a long time ago. I am merely worried now. Before, she always had a distinguished chap to lean on. But her last letter sounded…so desperate."

Alice smiled weakly. "It seems to me that despite all her gentleman callers, she leans quite a bit on you, Paul. Through the mail, I mean."

"Yes," he said, and she could see he was pleased at the thought. "I sometimes think that in spite of all her glittering beaus, I am her only friend."

Something inside Alice's brain slid smoothly into place and locked. That was it, something that she had been grasping to understand for a long time without knowing what it was: Paul needed Marie's dependence. He had once loved her. She had rejected him and he had been crushed. Yet it was her friendship with him—through the letters over the years—that had sustained him afterward. Paul was not a confident man, although a considerate husband. He had always faulted himself on not being as financially successful as the man Marie had wanted—and still sought. Even though Marie wrote about all those successful men, it was Paul to whom she turned, in whom she confided. And after all, she had never married.

What a fool I am, Alice thought. Instead of fearing Marie's letters and hoping they would end, she should be grateful for them!

They were saving her marriage. Without them, Paul would be full of self-doubt. But if Marie still depended on him, still (in his mind) placed him above all her "successful" men, then he was confident and content and she, Alice, was the beneficiary.

Events confirmed her analysis. As the weeks passed with no letter from Marie, Paul became increasingly anxious. He would enter the house and immediately thumb quickly through the mail looking for her letter. "I cannot understand why Marie hasn't written," he would say. "She was so anxious in her last letter."

"Maybe she will write soon," Alice would reply, trying to sound as if she meant it, for although she hoped for a letter almost as much as Paul, she feared it, too.

One dark morning, when a cold drizzle dampened Alice's mood and the trees, bare of leaves, were exposed to the winter wind, a letter arrived in Marie's handwriting. Except this time the writing was not bold, either because something had altered in the circumstances of the writer or because the rain had smeared it. Perhaps this sense of altered circumstance, or the rainy day, or various unnamed fears inside her caused it, but Alice did something which she had never done before. She opened Marie's letter.

When she read it, she was glad that she had. A second time she read it, more slowly, then walked to the garbage pail under the sink and threw the letter in. Over it she heaped tomato and apple skins, banana peels, and onion skins, in a felt parody of an offering to the gods of fate. She cut a perfectly good melon into pieces to make more garbage and threw the pieces into the pail.

Paul came home depressed. "'The day was dank and damp and dark,'" he quoted from somewhere. The water still dripped from his raincoat. He leafed through the mail. "Nothing else?" he asked.

"No," she said unsteadily.

He caught the note in her voice. "Nothing from Marie?" he said, an edge in his voice that unnerved her.

She didn't know what to say. "There was a letter from Marie…I seem to have misplaced it," she said dully, trying to sound convincing. She felt that she was squinting; it sounded so patently false.

"Misplaced?" He shot her a look of incredulity.

She averted her eyes.

His words came cold, colder than the drizzle falling outside that she saw through the window. "You threw it away, didn't you, Alice."

In all their years of marriage he had never used this tone with her. They had argued at times, but this voice was one she had never heard from Paul. It cut through her, made her feel cheap—like an object.

"I...I..." she didn't know what to answer.

"Tell me what it said...please," he said in a gentler, almost pleading voice.

She hesitated.

He touched her hand. "I know it hasn't been easy for you, Alice— with Marie's letters coming. Knowing I once loved her, I mean. I guess in some way I will always love her. Not like I love you, of course. You are much better for me. Believe me, Alice, I always considered myself fortunate that I married you instead of her. Marie and I are friends. I worry about her; she needs me. I...ask you to tell me what she wrote."

Still Alice hesitated. Then she sighed. "She wrote that she is going to get married but wants you to know that she loved you and will always, in a special way, love you."

Paul seemed to literally grow in stature before her eyes, though later, looking back to this moment, she could never be sure if she imagined it. He smiled and put his arm around her, drawing her close. "Thanks, honey," he said in his familiar voice. "Knowing that helps."

He was suddenly happy and relaxed. Her Paul. She was glad she had told him.

Taking out the garbage the next morning, Paul slipped on the grass still slick from the drizzle of the evening before. Out tumbled the tomatoes and onion skins and fruit rinds. He cursed and began to refill the container with his chapped, wet hands when he saw the envelope in the familiar hand. He opened it and took out the letter. The writing was damp but legible, the perfume faint and losing out to the wet, dank smell of its surroundings.

Dear Paul

This is my last letter and for the best of reasons: I am getting married. To Peter P. Jones. Yes, the Peter P. Jones (as the wags say, the "P" stands for "petroleum"). He is everything I wanted, everything that you, Paul, despite your good qualities, never quite were. I never loved you, as I sometimes sensed you imagined. You were a useful friend to write to between my "ups and downs." Now that I am "up" for good, I believe you will agree that it is time to dispense with your services. I need hardly add that now our social circles will be, to put it frankly, incompatible. I am sure you will understand, Paul, understanding being your finest attribute.

Regards to Alice,
Marie

Paul dropped the letter as if it were a melon rind onto the other garbage. He started to run back toward the house. Toward Alice. Toward a brighter future for both of them.

POOR MAMA

TONY BROWN

USAF veteran Tony Brown is an East Carolina University journalism program graduate whose fiction won contests by Union Writers and Art Forum and received honorable mentions in *Writer's Digest* and *Writer's Journal*. His work has appeared in *Foliate Oak* (University of Arkansas), *Vapid Kitten* (UK), *The East Carolinian* (East Carolina University), *The Write Place At the Write Time*, *Blink Ink*, *Gemini*, *One Forty Fiction*, *Whortleberry Press*, *The Storyteller*, *Down in the Dirt*, *Midwest Literary Review*, *Righter Monthly Review*, and *Short-Story Me*.

THE DESTROYER *SAMUEL F. JONES* IS ROCKIN' AND
rollin' as a typhoon bears down upon us from across the western
Pacific. Captain Jennings relays the order from Major Paulver to
Lieutenant Hill, who in turn barks it out to the top sergeant.

"Hit the nets and give 'em hell, boys...it's show-time!" Sgt.
Johnson yells, motioning with his arm over and over again.

I toss my foldin' money over the ship's railing so I can double-
cross bad luck, but watchin' it float down to the deep blue water
makes me realize that only means I'll be stone broke if'n I should
happen to survive this day. My stomach was already tied in knots
enough without them awful wind-whipped waves, what with
the impending assault on a strongly-fortified hunk of rock we're
about to make. The crash of the big guns is deafenin' as salvo after
salvo punishes our objective. Right now, I'm more'n happy to be
here, rather than on the receivin' end of that endless stream of
shellfire.

Got a feelin' when the enemy hidin' over yonder opens fire, my
idea on that subject will change mighty fast. So far ain't been a peep
out of 'em, though, and in one well-rehearsed motion we make our
way to the side of the ship and start descending the cargo nets like
an army of hypnotized ants led by the Pied Piper hisself. The landing craft is bobblin' like a cork on a fishin' line. I ain't a-likin' this
see-sawing none too much.

"'Bout time we got off this damn bucket of bolts," my buddy
Harper yells to me over the clash of metal and the crescendo of
cannon fire. Its sole purpose is to make that island look like the
moon's twin.

The pitchin' and yawin' of the *Jones* is such that even some of
the toughest salts amongst us are feelin' woozy. It won't nuthin' like
this when we was practicin' landings back in Hawaii, that's for *dang*
sure! Just as I reach the bottom of the netting and stretch my foot
out for the landing ship, two guys who have just gone over the railing above let loose simultaneously.

The barf that cascades down on Harper and me like grossly rot-
ten hot oatmeal is the final straw. Both of us upchuck, but at least
we have the decency to do it without covering our fellow Marines with

that load of manufactured eggs they called our "final meal" prior to hitting the beach.

"Final" seems to me to be a poor choice of words, in view of the hell we all are facing.

The LST we're assigned to has a small tank aboard. Harper and me are more'n happy to have that piece of *De*-troit–made machinery in front of us. This is our first time doing what seems damn near being a suicide mission, and we're none too happy about it, neither. We've both heard the horror stories from those poor souls amongst us who went ashore at Tarawa and Peleliu and such, so we ain't gonna be the least bit hesitant to hide behind that chunk of iron until the bullets quit flyin', believe you me.

LST 1205 must have a more powerful motor than ours—or a crew more eager to discharge its load and get the hell back out from the beach—because it's rapidly catching up to us. We wave at the guys aboard it and they wave back, giving us the thumbs up. They get the OK sign in return.

"How's your daddy?" one smartass yells at us, his hand cupped to his mouth.

"Dunno," Harper yells back. "Ask your mama an' she'll be lettin' you know, Bub!"

The boys on the 1205 howl; some shake their heads.

It feels just like a ferry ride to Cape Hatteras back home. On a rough sea, that is. So far, everything's as calm as it could be, under the circumstances. In fact, it's eerily quiet, even with every portside gun of the supporting U.S. Navy flotilla blazin' away at the most rapid rate possible—from the five-inchers of the destroyers all the way up to the 16-inch shells fired from the indestructible battleship *North Carolina*, God love 'er.

The beach is as still as it can be, except for where our shells are landing. Not even a peep so far from the Japs. Maybe they've already flown the coop like they done at Kiska in the Aleutians. Surely they'da let loose by now if they was on that God-forsaken chunk of atoll over there, where that volcanic mountain dominates the whole bloomin' island. Wouldn't give ya a plug nickel for the whole dang thing.

On and on we go, but still no response. The Nips *musta* bugged out. That's a good thing for 'em, too. Surely nothing could survive the battering that island's being given, courtesy of my favorite Uncle Sam. And that's *after* our flyboys done pounded the *hell* out of 'em for three days straight. So many palm fronds have been knocked loose that they practically cover the water all along the shore, sorta like a green carpet welcoming us.

The coconuts bobbing amongst 'em look way too much like human heads to suit me, but it seems that the day of my death—for which I made out my last will and testament last night—has been at least postponed.

Whether it's by the grace of God or by orders from the Japanese Imperial High Command don't matter a whit to me. The prospect of livin' through another day is mighty pleasin', either way. The odor of fried barf is the only problem Harper and me seem to face—that and the ever-blazin' sun, which is making it stink so bad even a damn turkey vulture wouldn't come within a mile of it.

The landing ship next to us has taken a two-boat lead now, and it looks like them fellers is gonna be eatin' coconuts and easin' under the shade of the few palm trees that remain standin' near the beach long before we get some relief from this accursed sun that never seems to find a cloud to hide behind.

A huge swell comes up as we're wavin' and laughin' with them fellers on the 1205, and all of a dang sudden the bottom drops out of the ocean—and our stomachs. Our LST dips so far it seems certain we're done for. I'm thrown to the deck, but up she pops like a cork out of a New York fancy-pants's champagne bottle on New Year's Eve.

"That won't good," Harper says, getting no argument from me as I check my arm bones.

I nod, green as a row of Carolina collards back home in Pitt County. "Yeah, man. What a rollercoaster ride! That woulda cost ya two bits in New York City."

Harper throws out that silly laugh of his, then looks off to port. His head cocks back.

"Hey, Roy! Where's the 1205?"

I grab a handhold on the rear of the tank and pull myself to my feet. Looking astern, I begin to point. "Right—" I start to say, but the word "there" don't never leave my lips.

The 1205 is gone. Not a single bullet yet fired in our direction, and already the casualties have begun. Harper and me scan the crashin' waves, but no sign of the 1205 or its cargo—or the guys we was jokin' with—ever comes to sight. The eager hubbub of small-talk stops.

My God! How quickly death comes, and for no reason a'tall.

One minute them fellers was as happy as clams and a-talkin' like us; the next minute, they was deader'n a doornail. Are we next? A shiver runs through me as I ponder my fate, but at least we're only a hunnerd yards or so from safety, and it looks to be shallow enough that even if the LST goes down now we got a good chance of makin' it to the beach that we previously were so deathly afraid of reachin'. Still, though, with the weight of all the equipment we're carrying on our persons, even relatively shallow water could mean drowning.

The boat relentlessly pushes through the surf, and we realize we're really gonna make it, seein's there's *still* nothing stirrin' ashore. We'll be the first to them coconuts after all, and with so many trees shattered by our Navy boys, they'll be a-plenty of 'em on the ground to slake our thirst and fill our guts. I can almost taste that sweet coconut cake Mama always cooks for homecomin' at Mount Tabernacle Methodist Church near Walstonburg. My tongue moistens my parched lips in anticipation of an unexpected treat.

I think I spot movement a couple hunnerd yards inland, and point towards it.

"Say, Harper, ol' buddy. Ya see somethin' off to the right at about three o'clock? Where that there cave is?" I nod for emphasis.

"You gettin' edgy's all it is. Ain't nothin' but a bunch of damn seagulls over there. We done gone through all this worry for nothin'."

"Tell that to the guys on the 1205," I say. Again I see movement at the cave, but this time I keep quiet. Maybe I *am* just seein' things.

"Keep yer noggins down, you lunkheads!" Sgt. Johnson says. "You may *think* you're on a Sunday picnic, but mark my words... all hell's gonna break loose any second now. The Nips are layin' low to lull us to sleep. They're there, believe me! When you hear a bugle sound out, hit the deck and cover your asses."

Despite the sarge's experience, most of us are skeptical that anything more dangerous than a coral snake is facing us, assumin' of course, that even a snake could survive this pounding. Surely, if there's Japs still alive yonder, they'da opened up on us by now. Even as the landing craft beaches and the front ramp smashes down, sending a geyser up and sprayin' those of us near it, not a peep is heard from the island.

"All right, you guys! Let's hit the beach and let's hit it hard!" the sarge yells, waving us on. "Move your sorry butts like there's no tomorrow and you just might *make* it to tomorrow! Remember, fellas. Those who hesitate are the ones that won't leave this beach alive. Let's go!"

With that, the tank lurches forward, surrounded by the landing party, with Corporal Wooten leading the way, Sgt. Johnson shepherding us from the rear. The coolness of the clear water feels mighty fine, shoving aside the heat that was radiating from all that metal aboard ship and sendin' beads of sweat down our foreheads.

Corporal Wooten, Harper, and the rest of the first wave throw themselves down to provide covering fire for the advance. The bombardment from the flotilla has proceeded from the shore to further inland as we approach, but even now there's no sign of resistance. Some fools let loose with a volley of bullets anyway.

"Cut it out, you knotheads!" Sgt. Johnson snarls. "After you hear Gabriel blowing his trumpet, you'll have plenty of use for the ammo you're wasting!"

The firing stops as the second file—me included—advances a little farther, only to find that the volcanic nature of the beach sand makes it so fine that it's difficult to maneuver in, even for the tank. Almost immediately it's stuck. Another tank comes to its aid with a chain and our tank is underway again, to our great relief. At least we'll have something to ride on when they declare the island free of resistance.

So many gigantic potholes cover the landscape from the 16-inchers that it's hard to believe anything could be left alive, let alone a human being. But, dang it! There's a sand crab right in front of my face, actin' as if it's business as usual. Just don't know no better, I guess. I hear a strange tinny sound from near that cave I seen before.

Gabriel's trumpet? No…a bugle! Sarge was right. We're gonna see hell today. In a split second a vision of my mother flashes before my eyes. Paw's a tough old bird, but what'll my death do to my mama? Look how she went on and on about Aunt Rosa and she won't even on Mama's side of the family. I hear the sound of hunnerds of rounds of artillery and mortar fire racin' toward the sand where I lie shakin' in my boots, but all I can think is, *Poor Mama*.

CAT DIXON

Cat Dixon teaches creative writing at the University of Nebraska, Omaha. She is the Marketing Director of the poetry publishing company The Backwaters Press. Her work has appeared in *Sugar House Review*, *Coe Review*, *Eclectica*, and *Midwest Quarterly*, among other publications.

When Mother was sick, Daughter ran
the place though she was the youngest.
In every litter there's a runt.
It can't fight to suckle.
Its squeals drive the sow
to squash, then suffocate
the blind piglet.

By the pigpen, Daughter would
stay for hours when the sow
gave birth. Which one didn't belong?
She read the clouds, the birds,
she knew: a storm's coming,
loud, thunderous.

She'd watch the piglet shrivel
in just one day, one hour
to a sun-dried, red raisin.
Still it cried. Waiting.
It seemed the right thing to do.
Pluck the piglet from the rest,
hold it by the wiry tail, then slam
the body against the brick wall.

Again. The eyes pop forth,
wild ricocheting bingo balls set
free from their cage; the blood
smacked and sprayed, an attempt
at Pollock with a bloated
paintbrush. Toss the body away.
See relief in the sow's eyes.

Years later, when Daughter learned she was
having a girl, she decorated
the nursery: walls, delicate green;
furniture, white as paper;
curtains, lacy pink, a crochet
of piglet tails; the rug hand-woven;
baskets to hold everything.

She waited with the patience
learned from the barn. Seasons
came to birth bright crops,
to harvest death: a cycle:
rain and sun, drought
and flood. During the long birth,
she lost so much blood, the doctor
almost called it, but tornadoes
twist away.

Night after night her feet padded
through the nursery door. The baby
wouldn't hush, latch, or sleep.
Her lips and skin so red
from crying, the piglet was
in her arms, a tiny oracle forecasting
a bad crop, a wolf on the loose,
a noose. It seemed the right thing to do.

Japan, oh! Japan

SONNET MONDAL

Sonnet Mondal is the author of six books of poetry including a poetry bestseller from Sparrow Publication and Authors Press, New Delhi. His works have been published in over 100 international literary publications including *The Metazen, Red Ochre Lit, Wilderness House Literary Review, Istanbul Literary Review, Red Fez,* and *World Poets Quarterly.* His works have been translated into Macedonian, Italian, Arabic, Hindi, Telugu, and Bengali. He was awarded Poet Laureate from Bombadil Publishing in 2009, Doctor of Literature from United Writers' Association in 2010, the Azsacra International Poetry award in 2011, and was inducted to the prestigious Significant Achievements Plaque in the museum of the Bengal Engineering and Science University, Shibpur. He was featured in *Famous Five of India Today* magazine and as an Achiever in the *Herald of India* and *United Magazine.* He has also been a featured poet at the World Poetry Reading Series in Canada and in *The Single Hound Journal,* Bruised Peach Press, the Asian American Poetry Project in the US, and *Andhra Bhoomi* newspaper in India. He was invited to the Struga Poetry Evenings 2011 to represent India in their Golden Jubilee celebrations. At present he is the managing editor of the *Enchanting Verses Literary Review,* editor of *Best Poems Encyclopedia,* editor of *Sonnets in the New Millennium,* and the Sub-Secretary General of the Asia Unit of Poetas Del Mundo.

The light tower rotates, probing for alarms—
Piercing mountains for volcanoes, oceans for tsunamis!
The Devil crawls beneath roads; air and rhythm from the sea
Kicks the tower off to slumber and cracks its legs with a sudden
quiver of panic—
Chains it with fatal silence…
A void of hush!

Crunch of leaves sets in, whirls into tempest,
Roars as shrilly as thunder in a cloudless sky,
Stuns calm Japanese hearts.

The unassailable approaches with a thousand watery arms;
Dinner soup in bistros of Ōfunato trembles in bowls—
Perhaps a mock-up of ensuing ruins.

Incensed waves burst out lives, seconds later.
Technology crumbles as thin folded papers
Thrown in a fire oven.

No one left to snivel even, for they float like garbage,
One with bricks, steel, and mud,
Smash against coastal lines
As if a myriad of fishes dead in oil spills.

A child sits on the back of the fallen light tower,
Her mind extinguished of hopes, desires, and ecstasy.
She pats on the inclined walls with soft hands,
As if trying to make it stand from death to reach the sky
Where the iron falcons fly.
All the time yet she fears to cry, fears to bleed…
Tears and blood may increase the drunken fluids.

weeds

SUZANNE ALEXANDER

Suzanne Alexander is a physician and writer living in Madison, Wisconsin. She facilitates a book club and writing workshop for the homeless and blogs about the experience at www.streetsofmadison. com.

STOOPING OVER HER GARDEN AT THE SIDE OF THE house, Clara clasped a weed and pulled. Her knuckles chafed beneath her canvas gloves. The sun baked the nape of her neck. Thick strands of long blonde hair escaped the bun at the back of her head and gently caressed her cheeks. Behind her stood the clump of aspen that she and her husband planted a decade ago. My, how they'd grown. The tallest of them was the nearest to her, standing like a sentinel, and from somewhere in its branches a bird chirped. Clara turned her head to locate the bird but the wind mounted and all she heard now was a chorus of rustling leaves. They had planted those trees in the spring of their second year of marriage. She recalled that spring fondly, so ripe with promise it had been.

The sudden sound of tires crunching over gravel sent her heart up into her throat. "Oh," she said, not meaning to. Clutching an uprooted weed, she pressed her hand to her bosom and straightened to look over the fence.

A mail truck idled out front.

She picked up her cane and planted it firmly against the ground before stepping with her right foot and dragging her left. She did this unthinkingly, rhythmically: second nature. The tip of her cane made gentle sucking sounds in the shallow mud as she made her way to the front gate. In her slow-motion haste she dropped the weed to the ground where it would wilt and die on the very soil that had nurtured it.

The mailman smiled tentatively and passed an envelope over the gate. Clara eyed the plain white envelope with suspicion.

"It's just a letter," the mailman said defensively. "A letter is better than a bill."

Without meeting his eyes, Clara took the letter in her gloved hand and retreated. She would have preferred a bill, but didn't want to debate the matter. Reaching the door at the side of the house, she paused to kick off her rubber boots and was surprised to feel the mailman's eyes on her back. It wasn't until the truck lurched into gear and drove off that she finally exhaled.

Up three steps to the kitchen. Clara settled in a chair. The cane rested against the edge of the table. She removed her gloves and studied the envelope. Even if she hadn't read the name she'd have known whose strong hand had crossed those t's, made the ink thick in unexpected places like the curve of a c, the punctuation like stab marks. Mason Field. *Doctor* Mason Field. The only man she'd ever loved.

Absently Clara rubbed the shallow indentation where once she'd worn their wedding band. Then, easing her lame leg into a more comfortable position, she remembered what the counselor from the Battered Women's Shelter had said: *Beware of sentimentality. Sentimentality is dangerous. It will make you forget. It will make you take him back. Don't do that. Teach him a lesson.* The counselor from the Battered Women's Shelter had drilled this into Clara's head daily for the entire three weeks of her hospitalization, and for the following three months during her rehabilitation.

But now, years later, with her cane resting against the table and his letter in her hand, Clara realized it had been a useless exercise; the barricade she'd constructed over the intervening years was weak, and maybe purposefully so. She still loved him. She must. Why else would she continue to live in the same house, tend the gardens, relish the aspen? She closed her eyes and silently surrendered to the emotions sweeping over her. She'd always known she didn't have what it takes to please the counselor from the Battered Women's Shelter.

The wind howled. A shutter banged against the side of the house. She opened her eyes, and then the letter.

My darling Clara,

I never meant to hurt you...the baby...You know this is true. How could it not be true? Certainly you remember the good times just as clearly as I do.

Father Bob has been my steady friend throughout this whole ordeal, visiting and writing regularly. He's sorry that you've stopped attending church and thinks it is because he denied you the sacrament of bread and wine. Do not hold this against him, darling. It is a rule that divorcées not be allowed to take communion. But perhaps we could reverse all this silly nonsense with a renewal of our vows.

Since you did not attend my parole hearing, I trust you agree that I've done my time. Eight years is punishment enough for a moment of irrational behavior, don't you think? I love you so much, that's why my reaction to your suspicion was so strong—it made me feel like I was about to lose you. And now I have. Or have I? That's the question I've pondered all these years.

Those other women never meant a thing to me...

I miss you, our house, our gardens, our life together. I'm coming home. You can send me away if you want to. The choice is yours. Meantime, I pray I haven't lost you forever...

Clara's hands fell heavily to the tabletop just as a train whistled in the distance.

Clutching the letter to her breast, Clara limped over to the kitchen window and surveyed the valley below. A Catholic church stood erect near the town center. Children played dodge ball in the church parking lot. Theirs had been a simple world, one that had welcomed and admired Dr. and Mrs. Mason Field...

Clara focused on the sound of the shutter banging in the wind, tracing it to a bedroom at the front of the house on the second floor, a room she hadn't entered in years. The sound transported her back in time, back to that black day—the flash of temper, the crush of his fist, the pool of blood at the bottom of the staircase, the empty nursery.

I didn't mean to hurt you...

The train whistled again and now Clara could see the black train approaching rapidly from the south. Her heart pounded wildly; her gimp leg ached. The question pressed in. *Did he lose me forever or not?*

Clara placed the letter on the countertop and stepped back to study it from a safer distance. The unfolded letter lay open on the countertop, as if in repose. The solid oak knife block, a wedding gift, stood stoutly nearby. Sunlight filtered through the window and reflected off the stainless steel handles of the knives. The shutter banged. The train whistled again.

The shutter banged and the train approached and her heart hammered against her ribs. Her mind filled with imaginings and memories.

Dusk. Dinner is over. Mason is in the living room relaxing in his leather recliner. Clara is in the kitchen washing dishes. The knife block stands on the counter, looming larger and larger, until she turns and withdraws the butcher knife...

Clara shook her head to chase the vision away and, seeking solace, returned to her garden.

In her garden she found herself surrounded by flowers: marigolds, lilies, and black-eyed susans gathered anxiously at her feet, their faces upturned as if they'd been searching for her. Clara spoke softly to her flowers as if they were children. With bared fingertips she gently cupped a flower and stroked its petals. But then, noticing an intruder, she cried out.

A solitary weed stood among her flowers and silently, defiantly siphoned nutrients from the air and soil. Its presence threatened the survival of Clara's precious brood. Instinctively, protectively, she put on her gloves and pulled the weed by its roots and, in the process, finally understood why she'd stayed in the home she had once shared with the man who had taken her child, her health. Realizing what role she'd play in the fate that would befall the once beloved Doctor Mason Field, Clara fell to her knees.

Birds chirped. The aspen quaked. The shutter banged in the distance.

Clara stayed prone in her garden a long while. Until the air went still and her sobs subsided. Until the moisture from the soil had saturated her dress and the weed drooped lifelessly in the palm of her canvas glove. Until she was empty.

〜

Clara dialed the cab company and requested a ride to O'Hare, the nearest airport with direct flights to anywhere but here.

"I'm sorry," the dispatcher said, "but that's the soonest our driver can get to you."

Fifteen minutes, Clara thought. *A life could be over in fifteen minutes.*

She pressed down while forcing the zipper along three sides of her overnight bag. She'd packed the essentials first—credit card, checkbook, and a copy of her birth certificate—and stuffed these between a few clothing items. She avoided the back of her closet where her wedding dress and little-used maternity clothes hung, still wrapped in plastic from the drycleaners. A thought almost made her smile—one day Mason or one of his women who meant nothing to him would have to contend with the memory of Clara, of crashed hopes and empty nurseries. It gave her an idea.

She dragged her wheeled overnighter down the hall and stopped to open the door to the nursery, a door that hadn't been opened in years. She reached in and flipped the wall switch that controlled the lamp on the dresser, the one with the base adorned with miniature carved wooden carousel horses, each horse hand-painted in pastels and accented in cherry—the lamp Mason had commissioned. She loved that lamp but averted her gaze, not stealing a peep past the room's threshold. She'd save that special torture for Mason. Yes, the counselor had been correct. Sentimentality was dangerous.

Clara hooked her cane over her arm, took hold of the rail, and began making her way down the steps, the overnighter slapping down one step at a time behind her. In the silence in between steps she heard a car door slam. She froze and wondered: had the taxi driver or Mason arrived first? Her future depended on the answer. It hadn't occurred to her that they might arrive at the same time. Had she thought ahead clearly, she might have taken a knife from the kitchen and kept it with her. But she had no defenses now.

Clara recognized the squawk and howl of the front gate swinging on its hinges, a sound the gate emitted for anyone who pushed against it. No help there. She cocked an ear and strained the airwaves for clues as to who approached. Nothing but silence. *He's crossing the front lawn*, she thought. Then came crisp, heavy footfalls as the unknown visitor ascended the steps and crossed the front porch. Through the sheer curtain that covered the glass of the front door below, Clara watched as a silhouette rose in slow motion into view. First only a head was visible, then a bust, then an entire man, a tall thin man. Had Mason lost weight?

The rap on the doorjamb gave it away. Mason wouldn't have bothered to rap. He'd have checked and, finding the key in its usual place—in the potted impatiens beside the door—he would have let himself in and called to her. "Clara," he'd have said, while setting whatever he might have carried up the hill on the floor with a thunk. "I'm home!"

At the bottom of the steps, Clara pushed the sheer curtain aside. He was a tall, lanky man with dark wavy hair and smooth skin. She recognized him, though she didn't know his name since they'd never actually met. He used to sit in the back pew after mass, head down, hands folded, as she and Mason followed the other churchgoers out the door; in this tight Catholic community, the slim Arab man always stood out and always seemed out of place. Clara herself had never ventured to say hello, a fact that had never bothered her until this moment. Of course, the rich white Clara hadn't been a cripple back then. She stepped through the doorway, dragging her bag. The driver smiled. He took her bag and offered his other arm and led her down the steps and through the gate. Clara wondered if he recognized her.

The taxi completed the circle and started down the long driveway, Clara's suitcase in the trunk, Clara in the back seat. She couldn't bring herself to look back at her gardens, at the aspens, but imagined they were cheering for her. She distracted herself by studying the back of the driver's head, and then the sign taped to the back of his seat. It contained his photo with his name typed below. Abdul Rahman. She looked up at the man again, at his hands gripping the wheel, and noted the absence of a wedding band. She rubbed her ring finger, then self-consciously fiddled with her cane, finally wedging its tip beneath the front seat while resting the handle against her good knee.

She leaned back and found herself entertaining an unexpected notion, of running a hand through Abdul's thick hair and planting a kiss on his neck. *Punishment for ignoring him all these years*, she thought. She closed her eyes but couldn't stop the vision. Now she was in his lap, probing the hollows of his face with her fingers, pressing her lips against his...

The car braked then, disturbing her thoughts and tossing her foreword until her shoulder strained against the seatbelt. Just ahead on the single-lane drive, a black car, a limo, crested a knoll, aimed straight for the taxi. Abdul safely steered his taxi off the pavement to let the limo pass. As the limo passed it slowed, then stopped.

Clara tried to sink into her seat but her progress was blocked by the cane's position. She watched in horror as the tinted rear window of the limo came down and an arm poked through the darkness inside and waved. A man called to her. "Clara!" Before his face could appear in the window, Clara looked away. She knew who called to her. It was Mason.

Abdul looked over his shoulder at his passenger. Panicking, Clara searched his face for answers. He raised an eyebrow as if he had questions of his own. Clara couldn't think. Her mind wrestled with images and emotions, memories and fears, dreams and nightmares. Meanwhile, Abdul waited. The engine idled. Why, she wondered again, had she stayed in the house all those years? What if she really did still love him? Wasn't it her duty to forgive?

When Mason called her name again, Clara shook her head. It was the tiniest of gestures, barely perceptible even to herself, but Abdul didn't miss it, nor did he hesitate to respond. He slammed the gas pedal to the floor and the taxi careened down the hill. Bracing against the back seat, Clara laughed. She'd never been taken so seriously before, nor known a man so quick to interpret and honor her wishes. When they reached the bottom of the driveway, Abdul turned the car to the right, toward the interstate that would take them to O'Hare. Clara rested her head against the window and smiled.

STORM DOG

GILL SHUTT

Gill Shutt is a Londoner who now lives in Wales with her husband, three children, and various animals. She is a sufferer of fibromyalgia and finds writing helps to keep her brain working, even if the rest of her is having a bad day.

Growling of the thunder hound,
All other noise beneath it drowned,
A deep and doleful warning sound,
Beware the lightning bite.

Frantic trees relay the warning,
Batten down and wait for morning,
Bringing peace, a calmer dawning,
Tames the Storm Dog's might.

Howling winds, the following pack,
Calling out behind his back,
As each one senses Storm Dog's track,
And howls to join the fight.

Lashing rain, their marker scent,
Telling all which way they went,
Then finally the storm is spent,
Until another night.

the coming storm

DAN DEVINE

Dan Devine is a scientist by day and an aspiring science fiction author by night, though he'll write any genre that pops into his head. His first novel, *The Next Best Thing to Heroes*, is currently available from Amazon.com in both print and Kindle editions. His second book is due out in 2012. Dan has had short stories published online in many magazines including *Dark Fire*, *Afterburn SF*, *Crime and Suspense*, and *Flash Tales*. Most recently he has appeared in print in the *Residential Aliens Print Issue Number One* and CyberAlien Press's *Strange Worlds of Lunacy* compilation. You can find out more about Dan's writing at mysite.verizon.net/dandevinefiction.

THERE WAS SOMETHING WRONG WITH THE CHILDREN.
The problem wasn't anything medical or chemical; the colony's fate hung upon their survival, and the doctors probed and prodded them daily searching for any signs of malady.

Nothing in the environment appeared to be doing them any harm, and with their strictly enforced diet and exercise, they were possibly the healthiest kids ever.

Their brains were functioning properly. There was no problem with their development, I was assured. Hell, I was laughed at. Their shared tendency to spend hours wide-eyed and awake, staring off into nothing, refusing to respond to everything from threat to bribery was no reason to worry.

"Children have never made sense to their parents," the other mothers chided me. "So they like to daydream. Who knows how we would have acted as children if we had been raised on a great big planet."

They were quick to point out that the condition wasn't shared by the slightly older children who had been born during the last years on the ship. It was just some artifact of a different upbringing, they insisted. I wished that our psychologist was still alive.

The only one who took my concerns at all seriously was Father Thomas.

"People will always choose to believe that which gives them comfort, Mary," he told me. "If the doctors say that the children are in no danger, then the other mothers will accept that as the truth and delve no further into the matter."

"So, you agree that the behavior of the children is abnormal?" I pressed him.

The priest shrugged, looking uncomfortable. I suddenly feared that he, too, was only humoring me.

"I agree that they seem a bit off," he replied diplomatically. "And I will keep encouraging the medical team to attempt new forms of testing, but until the results reveal evidence of some kind of pathological condition, all that we can do is pray for their health and hope that we are wrong, that it is some sort of natural phase that they will all grow out of."

That we are wrong. I thanked him for that, at least.

My own Evan was a lovely boy, with his father's midnight-black hair and my own ocean-blue eyes. He was well behaved, but still full of boyish energy—except when those strange staring spells came upon him and his face became still and somber, the gravity of his expression far too old for the body of the child it afflicted.

He was a gentle boy, always kind to the other children, and always quick to offer a comforting smile to any who needed it. He had a great love for animals, and they returned it, especially the crows that flourished here; he would feed them bits of corn and they would perch for hours on his arms and shoulders. At times, he would speak to them and you would swear that they understood him, for they would fly off or return, however he commanded.

He was such a joy to my heart that I knew I could never bear to lose him, not so near to the passing of his father. So, I watched with growing dread as the doctors tried the new batteries of tests that Father Tom had promised, and still came up with nothing. All the while, Evan's staring spells grew longer and came with greater frequency.

⤚

Days passed and the drought came upon us. The children now spent long hours in a trance-like state, often while congregating together. They had become a close group, still speaking with the rest of us, but keeping their secrets to themselves. Even the other parents could no longer ignore that something was wrong.

Unfortunately, there was not time to investigate the matter, as we were all much too busy just trying to keep our little colony alive. The entirety of my time was spent prospecting for new sources of water and helping to dig wells. They always came up dry, and I returned home every evening feeling a bit more exhausted and dehydrated than I had the night before.

I began to despair and sought out Father Tom for guidance. I was not the only one; the Father was a busy man during these dark days.

"Do not lose yourself to hopelessness," he told me. "We need only have faith and the Lord will provide for us."

"Your God is not with us here, can you not feel that He is lacking?"

Startled, the Father and I flinched in surprise. Evan had returned from playing with the other children, and we had not heard the door open. Even his voice as he had spoken those words had sounded as if it came from someone else.

"Evan! How dare you?" I scolded. "You will not disrespect Father Thomas like that!"

Evan looked for a moment like he would make a protest in his defense, then he shrugged and apologized meekly. He then went upstairs to his room without another word. The priest seemed somewhat unnerved by the encounter; our conversation floundered, and he left soon after.

Within a few weeks our extinction seemed certain. Our carefully planned searches, based on reliable scientific calculations, encountered no new reservoirs of water and gave way to increasingly desperate sorties into regions less and less likely to hold any. By then we were thirsty all the time, and could do little work in a day, regardless. Our dire efforts to filter the toxins from the seawater provided no breakthroughs, and our meteorologists' computers stubbornly refused to predict the slimmest chance of rain.

A number of the younger men and women gave in to their anger and anguish, constantly complaining about the unfairness of their short lives. In contrast, the colony's six youngest children never shed a tear, but spent their time together in an eerie silence.

Evan was rarely at home in those last days, and I awoke one night from a fitful sleep to find that he had already slipped outside. It was well before the dawn.

I found him, along with the other five, in the grassy open that stretched across the settlement's center. They were seated cross-legged in a rough circle. A crow sat on each of Evan's shoulders and a silvery-gray creature that looked like a wolf pup was nestled in his lap. The animals were unperturbed by his corpse-like stillness, but all three eyed me with suspicion as I approached.

I had long ago lost any conceit that I could somehow rouse my son from this state, so I simply lay down on my side amidst the grass opposite Evan. Something drove me to take care not to break the lines of their circle, a fact for which I felt foolish.

I may have dozed then, for the sun's first light seemed to break upon the horizon in an instant, and with it the children began to stir.

At some unspoken signal, Evan's wolf cub dropped from his lap and darted off into the woods that ringed the colony. The crows, with much disgruntled flapping, lifted into the air and pulled away in reluctantly broadening circles.

The children rose slowly to their feet, as if pained by old joints, but they made no complaint. It shook me to see them suffer so, no doubt from the effects of dehydration. They paid my presence no mind, and not even Evan deemed to look me in the eye.

Martin, Walter, and Shane, the other three boys, took turns approaching Evan. Each patted him on the shoulder and nodded to him wordlessly before turning and heading off towards home. Their silent, deliberate movements had the sense of a ritual and evoked in me a feeling of sadness. Carol, the younger of the two girls, displayed more childlike emotion, running towards Evan to wrap him in an energetic hug, then sprinting away just as quickly. I thought I glimpsed tears falling as she ran.

Maris, who was the oldest and tallest of the children born upon the planet, stepped forward and kissed Evan on the lips. This act would have disturbed me, given all the time that the children had been spending alone together, except for the complete lack of sexuality to the kiss. She gave the impression of a mother comforting her child. *My* child.

"Evan, what's going on?" I asked, my voice shaking slightly.

Both turned and looked towards me then, as if noticing me for the first time.

Maris opened her mouth to speak, but Evan placed a hand upon her shoulder to stop her. She glanced at him for a moment, shut her mouth, and walked away. I could not interpret her expression.

"It's nothing, Mother," he said. "They are just saying goodbye. I wanted to be alone for a while."

Evan placed his hand in mine.

"Can we go home now?" he asked.

"Of course," I replied, kissing him on the forehead.

I took him back to bed and tucked his blanket up under his chin.

"I love you, Mom," he said and was instantly asleep.

By then, the house was too bright for me to return to sleep myself, so I spent the early morning hours cooking us an extra special breakfast.

When I went to check on him a few hours later, he was dead.

Wailing with grief, I spun around and headed towards the door. I intended to search out the other children and demand answers from them, but I found them waiting for me outside.

"It is done then," said Carol sadly, after a single glance at my face.

I glared back at them and stabbed an accusing figure at Maris, who stood in their center.

"You knew!" I shouted. "Somehow you knew this would happen, and you did nothing to stop it!"

The five stood firm in the face of my anger.

"There was nothing that could be done," said Martin, the largest of the boys, sounding weary. His companions nodded grimly in agreement.

My vision blurred as my eyes filled with tears, and Maris had to tug on my sleeve to get my attention. She pulled me forward so that our faces nearly touched.

"This loss is not a meaningless one," she said. "His sacrifice will allow the colony to survive."

There was a peal of thunder, and I looked up to see black storm clouds sweeping in across the horizon.

Maris pushed past me into the house, and the rest of the children followed in her wake. I found that my fury had abandoned me— nothing remained, I was empty. I lacked the strength to stop them.

They went to his room, and each knelt by his bed in turn, muttering their sentiments too softly for me to hear. I saw that, like me, Carol was crying, but the others were as quietly controlled as churchgoers.

Walter, a tiny boy, even smaller than Evan, was the last to pay his respects. As he straightened, I heard Maris say from behind me, "His time among humanity has ended." The children bowed to him as one, then began to file out of my home. My eyes followed them as they made their exit; I could not entirely fathom what had just happened here.

When I turned back to the bed, Evan's body was gone. His clothing still lay upon the mattress, crumpled and empty. How could this be?

I slumped down onto his sheets and wept in confusion. A heavy rain began to fall. It hammered the rooftop and blew hard against the side of the house.

"Don't be sad, Mother."

I started, leaping to my feet with a cry. The voice was unmistakably Evan's. I glanced around me wildly. There, by the window, the mist blowing in on the wind was solidifying into a small, smoky form.

"What…what is this?" I stammered, stumbling towards it, falling to my knees.

Its wispy shape grew thicker, and though it appeared to be no more than a small cloud, I could make out the hazy pattern of Evan's face in its furrows and depressions.

"I am dead, Mother," Evan said, and it was him. "But only in a sense. In another I will remain with you forever."

Tears filled my eyes again, but this time I felt joy.

"How is this possible?" I asked.

The ghostly shape of the mist shifted, and I realized that my son was smiling.

"This planet was empty when we arrived," he said. "It had no sentient life, so it had no gods. We who were first-born here are bound to it. We will come to meet its needs."

I heard the sound of a storm crow calling from afar.

"I must go now, Mother, but I will come again whenever the sky fills with the clouds and the rain, and in between my love will always be with you."

I reached out to him, but the mist dissolved in the rising wind and left me holding nothing. By the time I had steadied myself and made my way outside, I was sure it had all been a dream.

The rain continued to fall, and everyone in the colony was out rolling in the mud, rejoicing in our salvation. I could not bring myself to selfishly tell them of my loss, so I simply smiled and waved as I passed. It was a long time before I managed to get Father Tom alone; people were exhibiting a rare inclination towards prayer that day.

When I finally told him my story, I found him less skeptical than I had feared.

"Who knows?" he said at length. "I must admit that Evan was right, I do not feel the pull of my Lord as strongly here. But it is clear that some force has intervened to save us all, miserable lot that we are, and it would please me to think that it was Evan."

My feeling of numbing emptiness was receding, but I had no idea what to feel in its place. I was worried for my son. He was a god now, but at the cost of a full childhood and a full life. He would never have a woman love him, never raise a family of his own. What would that do to him? Was it foolish to cry for the fate of a god?

"I know one thing," said Father Tom, breaking into my silence.

"What's that?" I replied.

"It's time for me to start spoiling the children."

He was looking for a laugh, trying to cheer me up, but he didn't get one. My God! Who knew what the other five might become?

ETERNAL

RANDY MIXTER

Randy Mixter has been writing since he was a teenager. He has had his poetry and other writings published locally. He has also written articles for a local paper and has won an award for creative writing. In addition to "Eternal," he has published a book of short stories concerning growing up in Baltimore City in the 1960s, titled *The Boys of Northwood*. His second novel, *Sarah of the Moon*, is a fictional love story, with a touch of mystery, that takes place in San Francisco during the 1967 Summer of Love. He recently completed and published *Letters From Long Binh: Memoirs of a Military Policeman in Vietnam*. That book is based on the letters he wrote home to his wife during a 1967 tour of duty in Vietnam.

SHE DECIDED TO MEET HER HUSBAND THAT DAY.

Well actually, the decision was made some time ago. It had been a year since Dan had died—slightly less than that if one were to count the hours and minutes. And Annie Warfield began counting from midnight until she fell into a restless sleep at two in the morning. The count continued when she woke to the first shadows of dawn playing across her bedroom window. The clock by her bed read two minutes past six.

Annie looked over to the pillow next to her, as she had done every morning for the past year. Usually, it was at this time that she whispered something to the empty space where he once slept. It was at this time, before the sun burned away the last vestige of the dark, that Annie told her husband how much she loved him, and how much she missed him.

On that morning, she told him about the things he might have forgotten. Small things, like the time he kept the Thanksgiving turkey in the oven too long, burning it. Then the mad dash to the grocery store to find a bird cooked properly. Or did he remember the day he had overslept and was late for work. He put on one brown shoe and one black that morning. How does one do that, she had asked him when he returned home that evening. The question was answered as most were, with a kiss and a shrug.

She remembered these things and asked him questions until the sun splintered brightly through the window's vertical blinds.

⌒

The day of their third wedding anniversary was cloudy and cool. It was a Saturday and they were still in bed at a time they would have been an hour into their weekday jobs.

Dan had inherited a prosperous construction company from his father and was a hands-on manager who enjoyed getting his hands dirty with his "boys."

Annie worked at a large bank in Maine, a short thirty-minute drive from their suburban house. She was a loan officer, which sounded important but really wasn't. She decided who was potentially eligible for a loan and then passed the paperwork to her supervisor, Edward Benson, who made the final decision. Annie rarely turned down any applicant with a hard-luck story, making Benson the bad guy in many a follow-up phone call.

Ed Benson didn't care. He liked Annie. She always smiled, a trait uncommon in the banking business. And, though he would never admit it, he had a schoolboy crush on his employee. He often fantasized about living with her. In his fantasies, Annie enjoyed wearing skimpy underwear and flimsy negligees around the house they shared and she loved to experiment in bed at night, and sometimes during the day if the moment felt right.

Annie sat at her desk, not far from where her boss snuck peeks at her without being too obvious, smiling as she wrote down the personal information of those in need. And when a story told from a hardship case brought her close to tears, as they sometimes did, she would look at the picture of Dan on her desk and her smile would return.

They awoke at eight that weekend morning, a compromise established between an early riser and a person who preferred sleeping in, but remained under the covers until ten.

Dan would usually hit the bathroom first. He was given a fifteen minute grace period before Annie joined him. On most mornings that was enough. Annie, on the other hand, was what Dan called a bathroom hog. She tended to take over the place when she arrived, allowing her husband the small area between the sink and the toilet. Dan worked his bathroom time with the precision of a fine artist; the consequences of tardiness were simply too barbaric to endure.

On their third anniversary, compromises and rituals were ignored. The bathroom went unnoticed under the darkness of the sheet and blanket.

"It's been three years, Annie. You remember the deal?"

She did. They had both decided to wait on children for a while after they married. Three years seemed like an appropriate length of time.

"I'm ready whenever you are," she said to the small patch of darkness that separated them. Then his lips found hers, and their bodies

joined, and neither time nor distance held dominion over them.

She left after lunch, under the pretense of grocery shopping, to pick up his present, a leather jacket he had wanted when he saw it a month ago at a local department store. She had talked him out of it then. It's July, for Pete's sake. Wait at least until September, she had said. But later that afternoon, she'd returned to the store and put it on layaway.

Annie returned to find a note on the kitchen table. Dan had been called into work for a couple of hours to assist with a new community project set for groundbreaking the following week.

Now there would be no need for stealth. She would wrap his anniversary gift and hide it before he returned and then she would begin work on his favorite meal, Annie's famous homemade chili.

She was halfway through turning the kitchen into a disaster area when the phone rang. She looked at the wall clock. It read ten after four.

"Honey, I'm so sorry," Dan said when she picked up. "This is going to take a bit longer than I thought. We can't locate the plans for section seven, and, on top of that, the material orders got screwed up somehow, and now I need to batch count the lumber."

Annie sighed and looked back at the kitchen. From where she stood it appeared as though someone had lobbed a grenade in there and then finished off the job with several sticks of dynamite.

"It's okay, babe. It would have been a late dinner anyhow. Hurry up and count your wood, I miss you."

"I miss you too, hon." There was a brief pause. Annie remembered that later. She remembered the silence as well as the words.

"I love you, Annie," he said before he hung up, and she said she loved him too. And that's how it ended, with words of love and Annie's famous chili needing to be stirred.

~

She was up now, moving to open the window blinds before she used the bathroom. She expected the day to be cloudy and cool as it was last year, and the strong glare of the sun momentarily shocked her. She no longer liked the days. They were too harsh, too real. Only the night with its gifts of shadows and solitude provided the peace she craved.

She left the bathroom door open when she entered the room. She never closed it these days. And when she cleaned the room, she never touched the toothbrush standing upright in its plastic container, nor did she touch the razor next to it. Those objects she worked around, careful not to disturb their place by the sink.

She showered and, when the glass surrounding her fogged, she waited to see his image, so real though sheer as lace, by the sink, cheating one last time on his fifteen-minute edict.

She had a light breakfast of cereal and, as she sat at the kitchen table, stared at the clock, trying to remember the precise minute when time had become her enemy.

⤳

The doorbell rang at 10:35 PM. By that time, Annie knew that something bad had happened. Not long before, maybe less than two hours, an emptiness had entered her. It had swept across her at first before making itself a home in her stomach, and then in her heart. It was such a feeling of bleak sorrow that she had gripped the kitchen counter for support.

"Mom," she heard herself say. "Mom, help me."

She was six years old again and the night was so dark, and her bedroom closet door was open, just a crack, but enough, and she heard something under her bed, something that breathed and scratched.

"Mom," she had said again, but by then she had made it to the phone. She had picked it up with both hands and slowly dialed his work number.

"Annie, he left here a couple of hours ago," the voice on the other end had said.

When the doorbell rang, she had been sitting on the kitchen chair, waiting. Her famous chili, which she never made again, lay cold in its pot on the stove.

After a while, when a hard deliberate knock replaced the chimes of the bell, she stood up and readied herself for the impossible.

⤺

In eternity we remain. Forever together. Forever in love.

She had found his anniversary present, a necklace with this inscription behind the silver heart that hung from its center. No matter the occasion, they always exchanged their presents at night, before they went to bed.

It almost went undiscovered, for she never moved his things, never touched them. She did look, though. Every day she opened his closet doors and looked, and that's how she found his present, a month after his accident, wrapped and ready, on the top shelf, in plain sight next to his folded work shirts, the ones he rarely wore.

⤺

The police detective—she believed his name was Alan—told her in the gentlest way that there had been an accident and would she please accompany them to St. Agnes Hospital. She could come with him and his partner, no need for her to drive. A priest stood behind them, a bible in hand. Would you mind if Father Carr came with us? And Father Carr, who had performed their wedding ceremony three years prior, came forward and gently gripped her hand. His hand—warm, despite the chill in the night air—gave her the courage of taking baby steps into the unknown.

She would remember Dan, not as he was on that night but as she knew him on the day they married. She identified his body by his left hand only, by the ring he wore.

Soon she was surrounded by all who loved her—her parents, her sister, her friends. They remained near through the funeral and the dark weeks that followed. Then they became as they had been in the past, as near as a phone call.

⤺

Annie returned to her job three weeks after. All of her co-workers hugged her and expressed their sympathies.

She tore into her work, arriving early and staying late. Ed Benson once again received many loan applications from his employee, many of which he could not possibly approve. He still peeked at her from behind the paperwork, but he felt a twinge of guilt each time he did so. He could not help but notice a small change in Annie as the months passed.

She had stopped smiling.

∽

He had been run off the road by a drunk driver, who was arrested on the scene. According to the police report, Dan swerved to prevent hitting the other vehicle. The cars brushed against each other, sending Dan, in his Chevy pickup, off the two-lane road. The Chevy struck a tree in a field, a few yards away. The officer who filled out the accident report estimated the impact speed at 60 miles per hour. It was a head-on collision which, despite the air bag activation, caused irreparable damage to Dan's internal organs. He died without suffering, the report read.

∽

She visited the gravesite on a daily basis at first. Sometimes she stayed for just a few minutes; on other days she stayed longer.

After a month had passed, on a cool November Sunday, she visited the tree.

She parked her car along the side of the road, a short distance away from the accident site. She left her car and walked across a field of grass and clover to the tree.

Annie saw the scars first. The gashes were deep and plentiful starting a few feet from the ground and ending at the level of her face.

She bent down and touched each clean, clear wound until she was upright once again. She raised her gaze to the gnarled leafless branches, wondering if the tree was dead or simply sleeping until spring. Was this what it had looked like as he had approached it? Was it still green with leaves, or the empty shell that faced her now? Was it odd that she found solace here with her hand pressing against the sun-warmed bark?

She wondered now if she had been talking to her husband at the wrong location. She felt him here at this place, this tree, more so than at the cemetery. His presence was strong enough for her to call his name, and she did this many times as the bark grew warmer still beneath her palm.

Her drives to the cemetery became more infrequent as her trips to the tree became more common. Annie visited the tree at least three times a week and every Sunday, no matter what the weather. As the days turned warmer she often packed a lunch and spent the day there, on a blanket, reading and listening. As it turned out, the tree was very much alive. She watched it as it bloomed from brown to a billowy green. The scars were fading too. Unlike Annie, the tree was healing itself.

By summer's end, Annie only visited the cemetery on special occasions, days that meant something to the two of them. The tree took up most of her free time, and as the days and nights began to cool once more, Annie made a decision.

〜

She looked out her bedroom window. It was a beautiful fall day. The leaves on the two trees in her back yard had recently begun their turn to red and orange, as had the leaves on the other tree, which she would see again soon. She watched as the sun lowered toward, then behind, the houses in the distance.

When she moved away from the window, she saw the house was dark. She turned on each light as she walked from room to room, stopping from time to time as a memory found her—but the time was short, and time now held great importance.

The house glowed as she saw it from her driveway. There was so much love still there, hidden in the spaces where they'd sat, where they'd eaten, and where they'd slept. So much love to leave behind.

But there was love in another place also. A love of the purest kind. A love that Annie had known once, so long ago. A love waiting to be rediscovered.

◡

She looked at her watch as she waited on the gravel by the side of the road. The time was 8:40—five minutes shy of the 8:45 accident time on the official police report.

In the distance, not too far away, the tree waited. From her vantage point, its silhouette barely broke the night sky.

She counted the seconds and thought of Dan. She felt so fortunate to be loved, so lucky to have been part of his life.

"Thank you for loving me," she said as she moved the car from the gravel to the road.

She gradually accelerated, then, as the tree neared, she pushed the pedal to the floor. The car picked up speed fast. She looked at the speedometer; it read 75. Annie glanced at the passenger seat next to her. On it was a box wrapped in colorful paper and topped with a red bow. Inside was Dan's anniversary present, the leather jacket he'd wanted the first time he saw it.

She gripped her necklace tightly, around the silver heart at her throat, and veered the car off the road. Ahead of her and above the tree, a shooting star creased the sky. It seemed to be moving toward her, getting brighter, so bright it illuminated the entire tree in its glow. And in that brilliant light she knew it was not a shooting star at all. And then, for the first time in a year, Annie smiled.

A STILLNESS SO
PROFOUND

ANN HOWELLS

Ann Howells serves on the board of Dallas Poets Community, a 501(c)(3) literary non-profit. She has edited its journal, *Illya's Honey*, for thirteen years. Her chapbook, *Black Crow in Flight*, was published by Main Street Rag (2007). She has had two Pushcart nominations (2004 for "La Resistancia" and 2011 for "The Madwoman cannot sleep") and one Best of the Web nomination (2010 for "The Madwoman caged"). Her work appeared recently in *Borderlands*, *Calyx*, *Magma*, *RiverSedge*, *San Pedro River Review*, and *Spillway*, among others.

The old dog paces, pads softly forward and back
across the porch; his eyes seek reassurance. Inside
cats take the high ground; Leila scales the refrigerator,
and Muriel curls atop the microwave, second choice.
Old Tom is nowhere to be found. It's mid-morning,
a summer's day, maybe a workaday Tuesday, when
the old man is scraping barnacles from the hull
of his small skiff; or perhaps it is Saturday, his wife
prepares for Bingo at the firehouse. Leaves
cease their tremble, sky stretches blue and cloudless,
birds have disappeared—no swooping, screaming
gulls, no twittering finches or sassy mockingbirds.
Swans, like tiny frigates, head for moorings. Noisy
hens that flap and flutter all day return early
to the coop or to roosts hidden deep among cowslip
and bramble. The world holds its breath.
No hum of cicadas, no bees in the hollyhocks,
even ladybugs fly away home. Snakes return to hollows
in the shed. Mice and rats, too, withdraw. They sleep
in nests of rag and straw buried behind rusted tools
and bushel baskets heaped haphazardly in a corner.
Flowers hide their faces, draw bright petals closed.
Squirrels return to nests in the old pecan; its leaves
raise silvery undersides as if in supplication to the sky:
spare us. Snails and periwinkles climb seawalls
and jetties, well above the high-tide mark. The old man
glances nervously southeast; this is the season,
and he remains vigilant. His wife, too,
notes the terrible stillness, draws buckets of water,
lowers windows, carries potted plants from the porch.
The sun puts on a false face, wan smile. The sea lies
dark and flat, gleaming with an oil-polished sheen.
No cars on the road. No boats in open water. The day
proceeds in slow motion under sunlight so flat it seems
a shadow play. A towering cloudbank materializes
far on the far horizon; soon the whole sky fills.

Slow wind builds, reeds and grasses kowtow,
prostrate themselves, mosquitoes and biting flies
blow away. When the first fat raindrops fall, everyone,
everything is nested, warm, dry, and if God allows,
safe.

the Rescuers

Ransom Noble

Ransom Noble lives in Davenport, Iowa, with her family. She enjoys playing board games, though she generally spends all her free time writing. Kids keep her busy, but she refuses to be separated from her books for long periods of time.

OCTAVIA CAUGHT UP WITH MALACHI JUST OUTSIDE the city on the road. "You were supposed to land next to me, not a mile away." She had seen nothing so far to tell her they were not in the right time as she traveled along the recently paved asphalt road.

"I get claustrophobic."

"I have to report you this time, Malachi."

"Not like you didn't find me."

"That's not the point." Octavia grabbed his arm to make him face her.

"You were a lot more fun before you became a stickler for the rules."

"The rules are there for a reason."

He frowned. "It's not like you ever lose me. You track me by GPS."

"One of these days you're going to land in the wrong time. I can't be wondering if something happened during the jump or if you just miscalculated your little prank."

Malachi had no response as they navigated through the town. "How do you think they managed to grow all this stuff? The grasses cover all the dirt." He crouched to touch the plants.

Octavia sighed. "Don't you ever read the project files? We're here before the War. This is what it's supposed to be like."

Malachi grinned. "Really? Why don't we relocate and stop worrying about it, then?"

She hated it when he teased her. While Octavia knew he had visited pre-War times, Malachi had not done so with her. "They don't have regular space travel. You'd hate it."

"Pity."

"And don't forget that most of the population would never pass for human by their standards. They've also settled all the untamed lands by this time, so we'd never go unnoticed. We have our orders. Let's get on with it." Octavia took the lead, navigating the city without use of her computer. "See if you can find the date. It's supposed to be March 15th."

"Year 2014. I do read the project files." He fell silent a moment. "Ever feel like we're stealing from the past?"

"No. We only take the ones that die unnoticed." She led him into an apartment building and climbed the stairs to the top floor. Standing in front of number 17, she knocked on the door.

"How do you know? Couldn't it be they weren't missed because we took them?"

"Stop being circular. If—"

A small girl opened the door a crack. "Who are you?"

Malachi raised an eyebrow. "We're looking for your mom. Is she home?"

The child turned and shut and locked the door on them.

"Only the ones that won't be missed, huh? How'd they miss the kid?" Malachi looked as shaken as Octavia felt. "How'd they miss the kid?"

She moved to check the computer, but the lock noisily opened. Octavia hid her wrist as the door revealed their mark. The profile of the woman they sought flashed through Octavia's memory: mid-20s, café-au-lait complexion, average height, slightly chubby.

"Can I help you?" The tired-looking woman held the door with one arm, sheltering her apartment from view.

"Angela Nichols?" Malachi's soft voice betrayed none of the shock Octavia had seen in his face from the presence of the child.

Octavia compared the woman's features to her memory of the photo from the file. She guessed Malachi did the same. They did not need to confer; Octavia could not question her identity.

The woman nodded. "Is something wrong?"

"No, we just need to ask you a few questions. Can we come in?"

Angela looked from Malachi to Octavia. "Who are you?"

Malachi had his business card out faster than Octavia. "Census Bureau. You should have received a letter from our office."

She scrutinized both their cards. "I'm sure you could ask from here."

Octavia frowned. She had not encountered such suspicion from anyone else she had visited in this time frame. The suspicion came later, when the government agencies tried to outmaneuver each other at the citizens' expense in the 2030s. She knew her history well; Octavia hated surprises on missions. "We're sorry to disturb you, Ms. Nichols, but this will only take a moment."

"Then you could ask here."

"It's rather personal."

"For the Census? I doubt it." Angela turned her head to shush the child who had started yelling inside the apartment behind her.

Octavia exchanged a glance with Malachi. The longer they stalled in the hallway, the more they risked the mission. She thought Malachi understood what she meant. "It won't take long, if we could just come in?"

Angela shook her head at them, moving to close the door. Malachi shoved against it, knocking Angela back. Octavia glanced around for onlookers, then followed on his heels as he forced himself into the apartment. He covered Angela's mouth before she could scream; the child made up for both of them with her terrified shrieks. Octavia crossed the room in three leaps, holding the child firmly enough to cut off her cries.

"Taking the kid, too?" Malachi looked amused.

"Do we have a choice?"

"Not really. Just making sure you didn't eliminate her."

"Stop it. You'll scare her, more than she already is." Octavia worked a sedative patch out of her pocket and ripped it in half. She placed one of the pieces on the child's forehead and held her until she lost consciousness. Grabbing a second patch, she hit Angela next. As the woman relaxed into a deep sleep, Octavia moved to look through the small apartment. "Watch them."

"As if they'll move now that they're sleeping."

"Malachi."

"I know, I know."

Three rooms branched off the hallway. Octavia checked each room—a bathroom and two bedrooms—but no other surprises greeted her.

He looked up from monitoring the sleepers. "Ever been on a mission where the recon was all wrong?"

"Not until this one."

"What do we do?"

"Take her. What else can we do?"

Malachi shrugged. "You're the leader."

"Malachi, I mean it."

"Most of the city will be destroyed in fourteen hours by the coming hurricane. Does it really matter?"

"Yes, if only to prove that we need better intelligence."

"Sounds like an excuse to keep a kid as a pet to me. What are they going to do with a kid? Angela at least has some value to us."

"The child might also be useful." Octavia dodged his other comment. He knew her too well; she had a soft spot for children since she could not have any. The pollution had left nearly seven in ten women unable to bear children, which was the reason for their mission to take those who would not be missed from the past.

"I doubt the girl will live to reach an age to breed. If she lives to maturity, it'll be a larger testament to keeping her away from the pollution than her genes are worth. The woman will be lucky to give us one child, you know that."

"Don't make me pull rank. She's going."

Malachi shrugged. "You're in charge, Octavia. You pull rank and I'll start calling you major."

"Just grab her. We need to get back before the storm hits." She didn't try to differentiate between the hurricane and the problems from their own time. They needed to get back before the time window closed.

Malachi lifted Angela gently, offering his wrist to Octavia to set coordinates. She hefted the sleeping child in her free arm, trying to find her balance. "Be right behind you." She programmed both of their computers for 11 June 2113 and Time HQ, then stood to watch Malachi disappear with their target. Fourteen seconds later, she followed with the girl.

Octavia wobbled on arrival. She felt older, though her brain told her she hadn't aged. The recycled-too-often air in the shelter felt dingy, stale. Breathing lightly, she acclimated within minutes.

She keyed her superior from her computer. "General Litken, Major Miller. Mission completed. Your presence requested in holding cell 082B." Her eyes fell to the child in her arms. "Code Green. Out."

"Acknowledged." The general's reply sounded off.

Litken might have been distracted or confused. "Don't think you're getting out of a reprimand because of this, Malachi. I'm still writing you up."

Malachi nodded, monitoring the sleepers. She hated his relaxed attitude; he knew she had trouble going through with the reprimands. She firmed her resolve against him, because the side trips had to stop.

Litken entered. "Code Green, Major?" His eyes filtered over the cell and its occupants. "What's that?"

"A kid. The recon was wrong." Octavia gestured to the girl, thinking how she'd explain her decision to bring the child back. Her breath caught when she noticed Litken's uniform. "Colonel?" Something had rippled. It was worse than bad recon.

"Right. We don't bring back kids. But why did you take a private with you? And why is he dressed in a captain's uniform?"

Octavia glanced from Litken to Malachi. Maybe the recon hadn't been all wrong. Something about the child had changed everything.

"Sir, the recon was wrong." She pulled up her report on her computer. "Look. It's from you regarding Captain Malachi. And you signed it General Litken."

Litken regarded the communiqué for a moment. "Fix it, Major." He glared at all of them in the room and left.

Octavia and Malachi exchanged looks. "Who is she to be this important?" he asked.

Octavia shook her head. She desperately wanted to see what else had rippled, but the longer they stayed, the more likely their world would absorb permanent changes. The time window ticked against her, too. They had to go.

Malachi let out his breath slowly. "Okay, so do we return just the kid, or both of them?"

Octavia shook her head. She gazed at the sleeping girl. "Just the kid, I guess. But when? She can't take care of herself."

"Whatever you say, Major." He picked up the child. "I can still help you fix this even though I'm supposedly a private, right?"

"You'd better. And no funny business at jump, got it?"

Malachi grinned. He exposed his wrist for her to program the coordinates.

She took her time with the calculations, setting his computer so he'd appear about a minute after they'd disappeared the first time. Whatever was meant for the child had to happen before the storm hit, so they had to stay until it happened. Recon had missed something: an overnight trip or a family connection. Someone should have mentioned the child at some point and given specific instructions for how to avoid her.

Her own computer took less time to program once she had the initial coordinates. She landed exactly half a second and three feet from Malachi in Angela's apartment. The girl still slept, and he placed her on the couch.

"Now what?" Malachi looked up at her from his crouch.

Octavia shrugged. "Your guess is as good as mine to figure out what to fix."

He watched her, then stood. "Wait?"

She glanced at the clock in the kitchen. The child wouldn't have issues with the sedative patch yet. "We only have a few hours. After that we'll have to leave her."

Malachi nodded.

She heard him going through the kitchen. "What are you doing?"

"Passing time. It's not like they're going to use this stuff." He gestured over the array of snacks he'd found.

She considered the implications before she sat opposite him. It was true, the food was not likely to be missed. "Make me some, then, too."

"Whatever you say, Major."

Octavia rolled her eyes. He laid out salami, cheese, crackers, and slices of apple. It was a feast only available in the past and she knew they both enjoyed every bite. He also found a couple cans of soda. She knew the caffeine would play havoc on their systems, but she savored it anyway.

A knock on the door interrupted them. She got up and pulled the sleeping patch off the girl's head, then let the little girl run to the second knock. Luckily the patch had few lingering effects for short-term use. As she swung the door open, the girl screeched her happiness at the woman revealed.

"Mama!"

The woman looked harried. She placed a wad of cash in Octavia's hand. "Was she any trouble?"

Octavia shook her head. The woman did not seem to notice that Octavia wasn't Angela.

"Good. Come on, Chloe." The two left.

Octavia sat down with Malachi. "Might as well finish, then we'll go back." She hated to waste the food. She was also in no hurry to find the future forever changed. Whether this worked or not, there would be no time to make more changes.

He chuckled into his hand. "So that's what happened with recon, huh? Wasn't her kid."

"Doesn't excuse them one bit. I'm still writing them up for the mission, too. Private."

Malachi's happy expression evaporated. "I'm not complaining as long as you let me eat."

Octavia nodded, lifting her soda can in salute. She figured the storm would hit in three hours, as long as the recon didn't miscalculate the time window, too. She hoped leaving the kid fixed the discrepancies, instead of compounding the ripples into a mess she couldn't fix. "Who was that girl, anyway?"

He tapped on his wrist computer. "Chloe is a very popular name in this time period."

"Well, she can't be related to you."

Malachi nodded. "I didn't feel different."

The food was gone too fast. "We have to get back. We'll look her up when we get back." She reached over and programmed Malachi's coordinates, then her own.

They re-entered the compound away from the holding cells. Octavia punched the partial name and approximate birth year of the mysterious child. She didn't look for the ripples yet. There was a risk any time they took someone from the past.

Only one match cross-referenced with Malachi's record. His first rescue from 2045 was Corinne Loxley, who had an older sister

Chloe. He had been supervised by Colonel Litken, who had then been promoted for the first successful rescue.

Octavia's wrist bleeped as the time window closed. Too late to make changes, so she hoped that everything else had unrippled when they put Chloe back. She and Malachi separated, to check in with the leads. She had a ton of paperwork to fill out for the recon team and Malachi's little pranks.

PRISONERS OF STORMS & TIDES

T. FOX DUNHAM

T. Fox Dunham resides outside of Philadelphia, PA. He's been published in over 45 international journals and anthologies and was a finalist in the Copper Nickel Annual Short Story Contest for his story "The Lady Comes in the Night." He's a cancer survivor. He is currently finishing his first novel, *The Adam & Eve Experiment*, along with two novellas, one a sequel to his published story "Inclinations of the Solar Winds." His friends call him Fox, which is his totem animal, and his motto is: wrecking civilization one story at a time.

ANNABELLE KNEW THE CAPTAIN'S FACE, RECOGNIZED it like a familiar map. She stopped her mind from pondering the source. She couldn't place it, but she associated his face with death.

She had dreamed of his austere face, his tight skin taut to his skull. In the dream, he summoned storms and flooded her home island of Whitepine, deluging the state of Maine, sinking the entire east coast deep beneath the sea.

The Otter Sound ferry had canceled its morning return trip to the mainland after a lightning strike electrocuted a pregnant woman as she bought a hotdog from the onboard vendor. The bolt had struck the radar dish atop the ship and followed the steel framework down the quickest path to ground, passing through the woman. A helicopter had landed on the island beach at the Lazarus Pier and medevacked her to Saint Mary's Hospital on the mainland.

Annabelle's fiancé walked the pier and proffered fifty dollars to any local fisherman who would brave the weather and its omens to get them to the mainland. He refused to wait any longer for news of Annabelle's biopsy results. She just wanted to go home, make some tea, put it all out of her mind. They found Captain Jackalow, sitting on the pier sipping from a whiskey bottle.

Annabelle shivered, sitting topside. Captain Jackalow forbade them to go below. Northeasterly winds whipped across the belly of Otter Sound, lashing the passengers on the exposed deck of the Century boat. Brian slipped off his black and red checkered flannel and offered it to her.

"Reeks of cigarette smoke," she said.

Brian gazed up at the churning sky, each vaporous mountain a province of storms. The clouds kept their own time, threatening to unleash their burden but biding time.

"How much time 'til we reach the mainland?" Brian called to Captain Jackalow.

"We're prisoners of storms and tides," he answered.

"An hour? Forty-five minutes?" Brian said. "I'm paying you. Least you can do is give me an ETA."

"You use time to control," she said.

"Probably about forty minutes," Brian said.

She sat in the back of *The Medusa*, her feet resting on soggy nets. She kicked away loops of crusty fishing string and some lead anchors rolling about the fiberglass floor as the boat swayed on the cradle of rolling waves.

Two weeks ago, her oncologist had spotted a mass on her annual CT scan—a test common for cancer patients in remission. He'd done a biopsy, and now they had to sail to the mainland to learn the results. Oncologists enforced a rule where they could only present such test results in person, so they could judge the patient's emotional state.

The last few days had taffy-stretched into long winters. Her fiancé had counted the days with empty cigarette packs. Sallow nicotine blotches stained his fingers.

The spitting sleet promised a winter storm. It waited just beyond the island hills—the gateway to the north, to arctic worlds where winter furies churned. The storm rallied strength and arms to storm the east coast, the soft belly of the middle states.

"Nor'Easter a-brewing," the captain said. He steered the boat into an avenue between a group of small islands in Otter Sound, probably following a route familiar to him.

Annabelle leaned over and undid her boot strings. She tied the left in a double bow, then tied the right. She tapped the toe of her Doc Martens several times, then she pulled loose the strings and tied them again. Her frilly white skirt waved like a gale-blown curtain. She scanned the landmarks, wondering if they were close to the spot where they'd consigned her mother's ashes to the whims of the waters. She had only frissons and glimpses of memory from her five-year-old self.

"We'll get there in plenty of time," Brian said. He sat next to her on the bench, rubbed her thigh. She gave up trying on her laces and let them flop to the side.

"Never enough time," she said.

"Mom's waiting at the pier with the car. She'll drive us to Saint Mary's. There's hardly any traffic on the turnpike this time of day."

"If we make it, we make it. I'm so sick of positive thinking and positive energy and all that positive crap. Don't tell me it'll be alright. Let's just see."

He lifted his hand from her thigh.

"You're right," Brian said. "I don't have a clue."

"Waiting is just waiting."

"We all wait for the Lord to come and take us home, by and by," preached the captain. "After the Good Doctor Sullivan cures us—the dark man himself. He cures us all in time."

She studied Captain Jackalow, still trying to place him. He looked like any of the ubiquitous sailors who lived on Whitepine: black pea-coat and cap, eyes glassy from cheap whiskey, hands gnarled from running nets. Yet she knew his face. She remembered its deep crevices like ink scratches in familiar handwriting. She recognized the pockmarks eviscerating his cheeks and forehead. He resembled the shadow man who'd tormented her nightmares—those night terrors when you can no longer discern the difference between waking and dreaming.

A vision bubbled up to the surface from her subconscious. She remembered him.

She changed seats, sitting with her back to the captain. She wondered how long it would take for hypothermia to kill her if she jumped into the waters of Otter Sound and swam back to Whitepine Island.

The boat cut through the choppy waters, racing the galloping storm at their backs. The captain turned starboard to circumnavigate a group of barren islands. Branches hung from the barren mulberry trees, sagging over the rocks lining the shores.

"What business is so important you risk heaven's finger?" Captain Jackalow said over the engine groan.

"My fiancée has a doctor's appointment," Brian said. He pulled a cigarette from the pack in his flannel pocket and lit it with his Zippo.

Annabelle kicked his shin, catching him off guard. He nearly lost his balance in the rocking boat. He grabbed the railing.

"Witchdoctors and medicine men—frauds. I've only known one of those blood-letters I could trust, knew him in 'Nam. The Good Doctor Sullivan. He cured the living of life."

"I can't take crazy people right now," she whispered to Brian.

"I don't mean to sound rude," Brian said. "We don't want to talk about it. You've already taken advantage of us. Just get us there."

Captain Jackalow tipped his cap and pushed the throttle. He cut the shore a little close, and Annabelle flinched from the rattle of the submerged boulders scratching the hull as they passed.

Brian paced along the edge of the boat. He finished his cigarette and blew out the acrid smoke. The wind blew it back in her face. She tasted the poison, felt it gnaw at her lungs.

"Such an insensitive ass," she said.

"I forget sometimes what you went through," he said. He tossed the pack over the side.

"I wish you hadn't done that," she said.

She didn't know what was worse: having her fiancé blow carcinogens in her face or dealing with him later when he went into nicotine withdrawal. To be fair, he had started smoking years before he met her. He didn't have any clue then that he'd one day be engaged to a cancer survivor.

He sat next to her, took her hand, stroked her fingers. His touch irritated her, but she let him stroke.

"We'll have a happy ending," he said. "This is just a big scare. Soon as your doctor reads us the good news, we can set a date. You know, I'm kind of glad we postponed. I'd rather marry you in the spring when nature is full of life. That's going to be our lives."

The circulation in her feet dwindled. Her toes numbed. She'd tied the boots too tight. She withdrew her hand from his and loosened the strings. She tied them again, but still too tight.

"How about June?" he said.

"It's so far away."

"Only six months. You could be a June bride. I know all little girls want to be June brides."

The boat rocked, knocking a Styrofoam bobber free. It rolled to her shoes. She kicked it away. It rolled back.

"I wasn't a silly little girl," she said.

"You do still want to marry me?"

She kicked the bobber with such force that it ricocheted and launched out of the boat.

"Let's just get through today."

"Let's say six months then," he said.

Sleet pricked at her neck, her arms. It whipped up into a proper rain, then dissipated just as fast. It threatened them with the potent storm to come.

"Och!" said the captain. He shoved a tobacco wad under his upper lip and squeezed out the juices, staining his jagged teeth brown. His eyes hooked her.

"Make him shut up," she said to Brian, grabbing his flannel sleeve.

"I remember this one," said Captain Jackalow. "The little one. A child so lost and lonely. Crying out for her mommy."

"Look," Brian yelled. "I've warned you. Leave us alone."

Annabelle raised her knees up to her chest and wrapped her arms around her legs, folding into a ball.

"She remembers too," Captain Jackalow said. "How could she not? Was this same coming storm. Same as that day when I sailed her family to cast out her mother's ashes into the sea. Storms are like that, you see. Fiddle-dee-dee. They're unique as people and live as long as there is ocean on the earth. It blew in without a care, to rack us with ice and wind then sail out again to open ocean to brood. Finally, it came back in today, it did—that same storm after many years brooding. Came out to see your girl."

Brian balled his hand into a fist. He readied to hit the old sailor.

"Leave him," Annabelle said.

"He needs to learn some manners," Brian said.

The captain grinned through his pearly shards. He spit the tobacco wad over Brian's shoulder and into the sea.

"Crazy son of a bitch," Brian said, pumping his fist. His face flushed red.

"Must you always be this way?" she said. "Don't you see me? Do you ever see me?"

"I'm sorry, babe," he said. "This asshole is upsetting you today when you're facing it all again. People like him think they can get away with it. I'm going to break his goddamn jaw."

Captain Jackalow paid him no mind, steering the ship around

another barren rock.

"Soon as we land," Brian said to him. "I'm going to teach you some manners."

She jerked down to tighten her shoelaces. She undid the right boot and wove a new bow but crossed the string and pulled a locked knot.

"Let me off," she whispered.

"What, babe?"

"Let me off the goddamn boat."

Brian huffed and rested his arm, releasing his fist.

"I'm sorry, babe," Brian said. "I'll cool down. I just want this all to be done with so we can get married. I've already waited six months."

"If you don't let me off this boat right now, I swear to God, Brian, I'm going to jump overboard."

She felt ropes tangled and knotted around her arms, her throat, cutting off her wind. She couldn't see them but felt their pressure, their pinching, strangling her throat, starving her lungs of oxygen. Her heart blew up like a balloon ready to burst.

"Calm down, babe," he said. "Look at me. I'm calm now. It's my temper. God I need a cigarette."

She stood up and gripped the edge of the boat. She held her breath and lunged over the side of the boat. Brian caught her arm and yanked her back, nearly pulling the bone from its socket. It throbbed.

"Are you nuts?" he said.

"Just get me off the damn boat. I've got birds in my skull."

"Fine," he said. "We'll stop for a minute."

He called to Captain Jackalow. "We need to make a pit stop at one of these islands. I trust you know a good spot. You've probably fished these waters all your life."

Captain Jackalow shook his head. "Been paid to drop two passengers off on the mainland. No stops in between."

"Son of a bitch," Brian said. He fetched his wallet from his back pocket.

"Extra stops cost a sawbuck each," the captain said.

Brian handed him a few bills. "Hope you're happy," he said to Annabelle.

The captain lowered the throttle and steered the boat along side a sandy inlet. Sticker bushes guarded the gate to the small island. Two dead mulberry trees with broken backs laid over much of the island. Their moribund branches grasped at the waves.

Brian took her arm to help her onto the perimeter rocks, but she cast his hand away. He withdrew, pouting, but he sucked it up.

"Stay on the boat," she said.

"Fine," he said, throwing up his hands for a second, shaking his head.

She found firm footing on a sandy bank and sat on the ruptured stump of one of the broken trees. She pressed down her boot, digging the toe into the loose soil.

"Just get the hell out of here for a while," she said.

Brian gave a mock salute then argued with Captain Jackalow. The captain throttled up the engine.

"We'll give you some time to cool off," Brian said. "We'll be back in a half-hour."

"I don't care," she said.

"Twenty minutes?"

"Just go."

"Ok. Twenty minutes."

She watched the fishing boat sail around the island and beyond, cut off from sight.

The sleet renewed, falling in clumps. She arched her neck, holding her bare face to the smothering clouds, the sun stealers, the dark vessels infesting sheer blue skies. The sleet pricked at her sensitive skin, puncturing like needlepoints, stimulating nerves until she grew accustomed to the sensation. Snow fell between the ice, melting on the water's surface.

Some of her mother's ashes must have washed up on this shore. She'd given the cancer to her daughter so she could die too. She passed to her the unfinished burden. If she'd asked Annabelle whether she would volunteer to relieve her mother's body of this debt so she could rest, Annabelle would have denied her. She didn't mean to be selfish. She just wanted her own life, her own chances. Not everyone could be a hero.

The wind blew low over the water, gaining speed, churning the snow into a frenzy. Thunder broke the sky and pounded the island. The storm blew in true now, the cold heart of it nearly encompassing the isle.

She already knew the results of the biopsy, knew what was coming—the storm that awaited her once more. She'd tell Brian she needed time. He'd ask her for an exact amount.

Time didn't work that way.

Riding It through

Bruce Lader

Bruce Lader is the author of four published volumes of poetry, most recently, *Embrace* (Big Table Publishing, 2010) and *Landscapes of Longing* (Main Street Rag Publishing, 2009). *Discovering Mortality* (March Street Press, 2005) was a finalist for the 2006 Brockman-Campbell Book Award. His forthcoming collections are *Voyage of the Virtual Citizen* (Lummox Press) and *Fugitive Hope* (Červená Barva Press). Winner of the 2010 Left Coast Eisteddfod Poetry Competition, Bruce has also had poems appear in *New York Quarterly, Poetry, Confrontation, New Millennium Writings, Fulcrum, Harpur Palate*, and other magazines and anthologies. He has received a writer-in-residence fellowship from The Wurlitzer Foundation and an honorarium from the College of Creative Studies at UC-Santa Barbara.

Canvas reefed and furled
we loaded the hold with ballast
as forerunning fetlocks
    and rearing frothshod hooves
stampeded over the bows

we scrambled to latch topdeck
battened down prisoners
    bivouacked in berths
havoc hatched us in grizzled
    sway of maelstrom seas
roaring winds swung us
    crashing under towering walls
of brackish avalanches

our steadfast cordages
windlassed to stave off disaster
    the hurled boat keeled
    to blackened sky
everywhere the compass
    spun our home-riven hearts
trawled for true bearing

we prayed a glimmer in vault
    a hint of headland
cutting the rim of horizon
    would steer us to harbor

oh yes, the poor

HAL O'LEARY

Hal O'Leary is an eighty-six-year-old veteran of WWII who now believes that the storm is upon us. Truth is as obsolete as chastity and accountability. The phrase "There is enough blame to go around" excuses all anti-social behavior. A complete loss of trust must follow, and when that happens we have a choice of oligarchy or anarchy. With over sixty poems and essays published in more than forty different publications in nine different countries, Hal was recently awarded an Honorary Doctor of Humane Letters degree from West Liberty University.

We are the reason we should fear the poor?
The distribution system isn't fair.
Is poverty a thing we can ignore?
When just a few demand the lion's share.

The distribution system isn't fair,
Excessive greed above breeds hate below.
When just a few demand the lion's share,
The pressure builds, and one day it will blow.

Excessive greed above breeds hate below,
It spreads and it cannot be wished away.
The pressure builds and one day it will blow,
And when it does, there will be hell to pay.

It spreads and it cannot be wished away.
The level of the misery will rise,
And when it does, there will be hell to pay.
Its consequence should come as no surprise.

The level of the misery will rise.
Is poverty a thing we can ignore?
Its consequence should come as no surprise.
We are the reason. We should fear the poor.

ᴛᴜʀʙᴜʟᴇɴᴄᴇ

BRUCE TURNBULL

Bruce started his career as a music journalist at the age of twenty and has since published stories on both sides of the Atlantic, most recently in *The Lounge Companion Vol. 2* (Lion Lounge Press) and *Halloween Frights Vol. 3* (Wicked East Press). He has forthcoming work appearing in 2012 through Rainstorm Press, Aesthetica Creative Works, and Bushwick Media. He also has a degree in English Literature and Creative Writing.

MATTHEW MADVIG COMES IN ONCE A WEEK; HIS MOTH-er pays the bill. Annabelle's office is on the third floor of a downtown walk-up. It sits above a bakery. Sometimes the smell gets overpowering. Matthew has grown up here; his memories are in the walls, like nails on which pictures hang. He is eleven now and talks mainly of his father. Annabelle listens.

On an April Thursday, he arrives at six. He tosses his gym bag to the couch and takes a seat. His hair is windswept and fair. Annabelle leans back and pushes up her glasses. They are old now. Like her. A framed diploma glistens at her back. She turns a wooden hourglass, sets it on the desk. The grains fall with a soft grace through the twist, like fine cocaine.

"Softball?" she asks.

He says, "Lacrosse."

In the silence, a clock ticks. *Tick, tick.* Annabelle scratches the date on a ledger. She looks at her six o'clock over the silver rims of her spectacles. He is not himself. Something has happened.

"How are we today?" she asks.

"Worse."

She says, "Ralf?"

Matthew nods.

"Tell me."

The boy lets out a long breath. His hands dance in his lap, a fumbling flicker of digits. He licks his lips, leaving a trail.

"Has he been to the house?" she asks in his silence. He nods, and she says, "Even with the restraining order?"

His confirmation makes her sigh. Ralf is supposed to stay away from him. From Matthew and his little brother, Calvin.

"When did he come back?"

"Yesterday," he says.

"Was he there when you got home from school?"

"Yes."

Annabelle waits. *Tick, tick.* "Did he hurt you?"

"No."

"Your mother?"

"No."

Carefully. "What about Calvin?"

There is a pause. A long pause. Annabelle listens to the sand singing through the glass. It sounds peaceful, taking its time like that.

"Calvin is sick," Matthew says.

"Is he okay?"

Matthew lowers his head. There is a look about him of a carnation on the soil of a freshly dug grave. The blinds are closed to what is left of the sun; coldness seeps through the cracks. The building is old, like her glasses—like her. She imagines Calvin and the smell of linoleum tile, the sound of a siren. Doctors pushing on.

It kills her. Three years old, damnit. *Three.*

"He went to the hospital," Matthew says. "Dad got arrested."

"They let him out?"

A shrug. "Don't know. Maybe."

"What did he do?"

"Shook him up."

"Like with you?" she asks.

"Yeah," he says, looking away. "Calvin never cried like that before."

Annabelle sits forward, the leather creaking beneath her. "He still works at The Oriental, right?"

"Sometimes. I don't think he'll last. He's always late."

"He told you this?"

He shrugs again. It was his mother who told him; she is sure about that. The woman is still sleeping with Ralf. The separation isn't working.

"He's having an affair," Matthew says.

"Do you know the woman?"

"No," he says. "But she's no good for him."

Annabelle agrees. It should be raining outside. In her tight little office, she feels an oncoming storm.

"What happened last night, Matt?"

The boy frowns. "Dad was home, making dinner in the kitchen. He shouldn't have been there. He was shouting; he couldn't get the recipe right. Calvin was crying upstairs. Wouldn't stop. Dad threw a fry pan to the floor. It clattered."

Annabelle taps her pen against the ledger: *click, click*.

"How did he seem?"

"Bad," Matthew says. "Worse than February."

She understands. February was a cold month. Ralf Madvig hit Matthew with a tire iron then. He was rotating his tires when it happened. Matthew was supposed to help, but couldn't. Small hands. Weak and gauche. He had to go to St. John's in the end. Ralf was arrested. First strike. Annabelle visited Matthew in the hospital. She remembers the mark of the iron, like a dark continent.

"How did it escalate?" Annabelle asks.

Shades pass over his face, like shadows on water. "He threw the pan with the food in it. Rice, vegetables—it all rolled on the floor. Calvin was crying."

"And your mother?"

"She was in the living room," he says. "Too scared to move. Dad went up to see Calvin. He shouldn't have been there."

"Why did she let him in?"

The boy sighs, kicks his feet. "She loves him, I guess. She's dumb."

"And Calvin? What happened to him?"

"Dad tried too hard to make him stop. While he was up there, I covered my ears. It got loud. Calvin is a good kid. Never heard him cry like that before."

"He dislocated your shoulder," Annabelle says. "When you were five."

She watches for a change in his features. If the memory is painless now, it's because it is buried beneath the skin.

"He'll kill Calvin," he says, in a spectral way. Annabelle doesn't want to admit he is probably right.

"You say he shook him. Did the doctors tell you that?"

"No, I knew," Matthew says. "It's his style."

In the shuffle of his fingers, she sees raw skin spiking his knuckles. He catches her eye and his look explains it all.

"You hit him," she says.

"So? You gonna give me a lecture?"

She sits back, takes him in. The boy looks harder now, like a man. He is eleven and violent. He has been taught this by his father. His mother is a wreck, a drunk, a waste. She doesn't see her son growing to fill a shadow, to walk in bloody footsteps. She will die knowing she let a brute destroy her family. Meanwhile, his father sleeps with two women; he has a choice.

"When did you hit him?" she asks.

"When he came downstairs. Calvin was quiet then. In the kitchen, the dog was eating our dinner. I picked up the pan. Dad looked so hard at me, like he was trying to figure something out. I called him a bad word. He tried to get me. I used the pan."

"What about your knuckles?"

He doesn't check them. "I hit him again when the pan flew out of my hand. On the face. He's black now."

Annabelle lets the image float away. "Your mother called the police?"

"Had to," he says. "Dad wanted to kill her and me. I thought he'd already done it to Calvin. He wasn't arrested right away. He ran, I think. To his other girlfriend."

A minute goes by. Matthew smiles at some distant joy and says, "We won at lacrosse."

At least there's that, Annabelle thinks, and notices the doughy smell coming up from the floor, like the perfume of the dead.

⌒

The manager at The Oriental gives Ralf Madvig five minutes for his break. He has a visitor in the window booth. She wears glasses and a brown duffle. Ralf throws a towel over his shoulder and takes the seat across from her. His gray eyes dart about the restaurant. The air is fried rice and steam. Someone speaks Chinese.

"What are you doing, Ralf?"

"Working," he says.

Annabelle smiles. "You know what I'm talking about."

He tries to escape her look. "You're not my shrink."

"But I speak to your boy," she says. "He's hurting. He told me you were arrested. Said you broke Calvin."

"Hey, watch what you say."

She leans forward. The man's left eye shakes.

"When is it going to stop, Ralf?"

For the first time his eyes leave hers. They drop to his hands, clasped together, like Matthew's in her office.

"They had it coming," he says, and Annabelle feels compelled to strike him. Inside, a demon rages.

"You can't keep on," she says.

"It's not like I planned it."

She sighs and watches as a couple walk through the doors. The guy has his arm around a teenage waist; the girl laughs at an unheard joke.

"Does she know about us?" Annabelle asks.

He knows she means his wife. "Not really."

"Meaning?"

"She knows I'm screwing someone else. What of it?"

"I think Matthew is going south," she says. "Also…this isn't working."

In a flash, she senses an eruption. Ralf has that look about him, like the vicious wind that strips an airplane of its safety.

"You wanna break it off?" he asks.

"It's too dangerous," she says.

His laughter is like the cackle of a witch. "Ain't that what you like about it?"

And it's strange how deep he can penetrate her, even now. A grin spreads on his dark-stubbled face; he has scored a point (*we won at lacrosse*).

The softness of his hand against hers is nylon to shaven legs.

"They let me out," he says. "Can't be as bad as all that."

"But your children," she says.

"I know. They just don't get it."

She frowns. "Don't get what?"

"Everything," he says. "They do everything *wrong*."

She is appalled. "That's no reason to beat on them."

Ralf hates the idea of being a bad man. She can see it in his blackened face, in the way his fists clench.

"I could get you some help," she says. "I know people."

He runs his palms over his face. An outburst occurs. "Don't wanna talk to no shrink!"

"But you can't go on like this. You will go to jail."

Again he says, "Watch what you say!"

Another waiter approaches. Ralf hears, "You got table nine."

He throws his fist down and the customers jump. Annabelle stays still, though her heart beats a bossa nova.

"Gimmie one minute," he says to the waiter.

"Ralf," she says.

And the waiter says, "Get to it now, Madvig!"

He breaks before her. "Goddamnit!" he says, and throws an aimless punch. Her glasses fly; they crack on the stone floor. Someone gasps.

The air is steam.

Holding her cheek, she looks at him but doesn't cry.

"You'd better get to work," she says.

He gets up, ripping a pad from his apron, and turns to table nine, asking the twitching customers what they want.

On her way out, she sees the manager dialing the phone. He is looking over at Ralf, who stands like a statue before the table. Annabelle can't hear the manager, but she reads his lips. He is talking quietly, trying not to be heard.

～

They have an appointment scheduled for six on Thursday; Annabelle can't make it. At the park, she hears the scuffle of a game in progress. Under the evening sky, the boys and their white uniforms are chessboard pieces. Someone has played with them all, one way or another.

When it is over, Matthew catches her eye. She waves him closer; he comes. She doesn't know why she feels the need to tell him now, of all times.

It seems the right thing to do.

"How did it go?" she asks.

Panting, he says, "We lost."

"I can't see you tonight," she says.

There is a passing look of regret. "Oh?"

"I need to come clean about something."

He looks concerned.

And when she tells him, she sees Ralf in his face, in his eyes. A friend calls from the grass; they are going for pizza.

"Sorry about Calvin," she says. "I'll be there on Sunday."

She has to walk away now. He calls after her. Blaming her, of course. Ralf blew his chance with that kid. Blew it all to hell.

In the dust of a truck, she walks, thinking of Calvin. The vehicle is carrying baked goods. She breathes in its foul and funereal fragrance.

Perfume of the dead.

TWISTER

JOE MASSINGHAM

Joe Massingham was born in the UK but has lived half his life in Australia. He retired early because of cancer and heart problems and now spends his time waiting to see doctors and writing. He has been published in Australia, New Zealand, India, Ireland, the UK, and the US.

EDITOR'S NOTE: The typographic layout of this poem is very important, but results in a small type size. A larger version of the poem's text is included on page 206.

If you glanced up at the right moment you might think you had a dust speck in your eye,
or perhaps a nervous tic, because you thought you'd seen a little flicker in the cloud
that was building in the springtime sky and you'd go about your business without a
second glance. But you'd be wrong. The flicker, quicker than you'd imagine
possible, would transform itself into a little twirling spinning top in the
center of the cloud, the balance point on which it stood resting on
the unseen floor that held the cloud in place. And if you'd kept
watching you would have seen the spinning spiral lengthen
until it reached all
the way from
heaven to
unsuspecting
earth
as if it was
reluctant
to move
but was
being
pulled
along
by the cloud
gathering
speed as
it looked
for somewhere
where it could clear
a convenient place
on which it could spread its
aching twisted limbs so they could pull their punches, finally falling asleep on a dusty
sofa, leaving disoriented, dislocated folk to mourn lost harvests, homes—heartbreak.

natural selection

William Rasmussen

Since March of 2010, William "Bill" Rasmussen has had short tales of horror published at *Sounds of the Night*, *Fantastique Unfettered*, *The Absent Willow Review*, *parABnormal Digest*, *Black Ink Horror*, *Midnight Street*, *Bête Noire*, and *The Horror Zine*. His digital collection, *Claw Marks & Other Disturbing Diversions*, was released by Crossroad Press in September of 2010, and is available at Amazon. His novella, *Infinity Twice Removed*, co-written with Michael McBride, was released in hardcover by Delirium Books in December of 2011 as part of their HC Novella Line. Bill is a retired FBI agent who currently resides just outside of Memphis, TN, with his loving wife.

THE HOMELESS MAN'S THROAT HAD BEEN CUT VIRTU-
ally from ear to ear, and deep enough that Detective Russell Gregory could glimpse a portion of the man's spine. *My God*, he thought,
what's the world coming to? He flipped his small notebook closed
with a shake of his head and watched as the ambulance attendants
covered the body with a white sheet, preparatory to hauling away
the remains.

Thirty-eight years old, tall, black, and single, Gregory had been
a detective with the Memphis Police Department for ten years now,
and in the hot bed of the south he'd seen a lot of atrocities during that time. Black on white crime, white on black crime, black
on black crime—you name it. But this was just getting ridiculous.
The elderly white man lying enshrouded on the curb—like a bag of
garbage—atop a pool of blood at the corner of Danny Thomas and
Court was the third victim in a string of brutal murders centered in
the heart of downtown Memphis, TN, in just over two weeks. Same
MO: a sudden, violent attack late at night on a weak, elderly homeless man, the coup de grâce being a vicious knife slash to the throat
causing the victim to bleed out in mere seconds. No witnesses, no
leads, little, if any, forensic evidence thus far, and, therefore, no sus-
pects. He was no closer to solving this case now than he was after
the first victim, a crippled black man, felt the killer's knife.

Gregory stepped away from the body and gazed east to where the
sun was just peeking over the tops of the mid-town low-rises. He
sighed, realizing it was going to be a long day.

↜

"I'm telling you, man, sumthin's wrong!" the wizened, slightly
inebriated derelict said. "It's not li' Bill to jes' up and walk away li'
dat."

Detective Joe Donnelly pulled away from the sour odor of wine
swirling about the man like rank perfume and nodded his head
in agreement. He'd been tasked to interview the "transient" after
fielding a call from a Shelby County Sheriff's Office deputy who
had been flagged over by the elderly white man on I-40, near the

outskirts of the county. The guy had raved on and on to the deputy, like a wild man, about his missing friend, with whom he had shared a safe, fairly discreet sleeping spot the last several nights beneath an overpass on the interstate. Donnelly was currently standing alongside his late-model Chevy Impala, near mile marker 25 off of I-40 West, where the two guys had spent the previous evening under the overpass on the canted concrete support in their sleeping bags, trying to elicit additional details from the feisty old-timer.

"So you're sure this buddy of yours wouldn't simply have taken off without letting you know?"

"I'm pos'tive," the elderly man said. "We was tight, y'know?"

"Yeah," Donnelly said with some degree of doubt, stepping away and staring closely about the vicinity where the two men had spent the night. Nothing of note, he noticed, just his interviewee's tattered sleeping bag lying atop the sloping concrete foundation beneath the Airline Road overpass and some of their fast-food trash. Scanning either side of the embankment, however, he was surprised to see a thick profusion of lengthy, green trailing vines completely surrounding the location and encroaching on the canted foundation itself.

"Damn kudzu," he mumbled.

The vine had been introduced from Japan into the southeastern United States in the late 1800s as a foraging crop and to help prevent soil erosion. Unfortunately, it was only much later that farmers learned how quickly it spread, how destructive it was—climbing up wires, trees, poles, virtually anything standing, or choking and smothering whatever vegetation it infested—and how difficult it became to contain or eradicate. It soon earned the demeaning nickname "the vine that ate the South." Donnelly even recalled reading somewhere that kudzu could grow at the rate of a foot a night. *Unbelievable!* he thought.

He turned his attention back to the homeless man, asked him for a name and description of his missing friend, and jotted the information down in his notebook. He slapped closed his pad and trudged in the direction of his car. He sighed; he was tired. Only 9:30 in the morning, the temperature was already 85 degrees and it was just the first week of May! He was forty years old, a shade under six feet tall, was carrying an extra twenty pounds around his middle like a small inner tube, which made him one seriously out-of-shape white guy, and he was recently divorced. *Some life*, he thought, sliding behind the wheel of his unmarked cruiser.

Pulling out of the breakdown lane and away from the scene, he merged easily with the spotty interstate traffic and wondered if there was anything to the recent rash of disappearances—this incident brought the total to four—of homeless men along I-40.

⤸

"Rough day, huh?" Donnelly said, topping off his friend's glass of beer from their pitcher.

"Shit, it couldn't get much worse," Gregory replied, shaking his head.

The two detectives were sitting at a side table at their favorite watering hole, T. J. Mulligan's, situated just inside the Memphis city limits, beyond which Shelby County stretched. It was a little after 7:00 that evening, and the pair had decided to meet for drinks, as they did fairly often, to discuss their trying days and compare notes. They had both graduated from the University of Memphis back-in-the-day, missing each other by a couple of years. But fate intervened about ten years ago when they bumped into each other while enrolling in a few courses in Criminal Justice at Southwest Tennessee Community College. Since then they had become fast friends, despite their different racial backgrounds. Donnelly firmly believed that if it hadn't been for his buddy's unwavering support during his recent divorce, he just might have eaten his gun.

"Another slasher killing this morning," Gregory said between sips. "A bad one."

"Damn!" Donnelly said. "What's that make…three? Any leads?"

"Nope. Damn frustrating is what it is." He paused. "Sickening too."

"I'll bet," Donnelly said, thinking. "I told you I had another report of a missing guy off the interstate this morning, right? Really strange…"

"Why d'you say that?"

"I don't know…" Donnelly said. "Just not sure whether to believe these guys who report it. They claim to be 'buddies'"—he put his hands in the air, fingers curled, to mimic quotation marks—"with the missing men, but how do I know if they were actually that close to believe their story, or their concern? I mean, for all I know, the missing guys just got tired of tagging along with someone else and bolted during the night."

"Yeah," Gregory said. "I see where you're coming from, my man."

"Somethin' else too…" Donnelly began.

"What?"

"Ahhh, it's nothing…Don't worry about it."

Gregory stared at his friend for a moment, his brow furrowed.

They sipped their beers in silence for a few minutes, unwinding to the rock and country music alternately spilling out of the bar's muted sound system, letting the alcohol work its magic.

"Any hit on the description of the homeless man I gave you this morning?" Donnelly said abruptly.

"Nah, sorry man. Forgot to tell you."

"No prob. Just keep your ears open, huh?"

"Will do."

The two of them chatted on for another hour or so about less grisly or troublesome subjects before deciding to call it an early night. They promised to check in with each other in the next day or two.

⌐

A few days later Gregory made the scene at yet another early morning homicide, courtesy of the "City Slasher," as the Memphis *Commercial Appeal*, the city's lone daily, had dubbed the serial killer. The fourth killing featured the same MO: a lone, elderly homeless man surprised on the street in the wee hours by an unknown assailant, his throat slashed viciously, with death occurring virtually seconds later. And, coming as no surprise to the seasoned detective, there were no leads and no witnesses, the only difference being that the crime took place in the mid-town area, some four or five miles east of the downtown district.

❧

That same afternoon, on a hunch, Donnelly revisited the various places where of late four vagrants had been reported missing. He didn't know what he was looking for exactly, only that something subconsciously bothered him about the area where the last man had "disappeared." But after canvassing all four locations and coming up empty, he became more frustrated than ever. There was simply nothing of significance to be found at the sites, other than rubbish and litter left by their previous tenants or thoughtless interstate travelers. For what it was worth, however, two small items of note did strike him as decidedly odd. First off, the ground immediately surrounding the area of all four "disappearances" had become positively saturated with kudzu, so much so that the vines had even slithered like drowsy snakes onto the sloping concrete, which many homeless men had apparently called home, if only for the night. Second, the locations on the interstate where the aged vagrants had reportedly gone "missing" were slowly shifting mile by mile to the west, inexorably advancing toward the city.

❧

That evening after work, Gregory and Donnelly were huddled together once again at T. J. Mulligan's, sipping long-necks, relaxing, inhaling the enticing aromas circulating throughout the restaurant/bar, and discussing their current, baffling cases.

"I don't know, Joe…after four murders I've still got almost nothing to go on. I need a frickin' break in this case."

"I know what you mean," Donnelly said, tipping back his bottle of beer. "You've at least got forensics on the murder weapon, right?"

"Yeah, the perp caught the victim's spine twice," Gregory said, discouraged nevertheless. "But a lot of good it does without a suspect or the blade."

"Yeah," Donnelly mumbled, nodding his head in agreement. "Hang in there, man, you'll catch a break soon."

"I hope so," Gregory said. He paused then, bottle poised before his lips. "What's happening in your corner of the world? Any developments on your homeless 'abductions?'" he chuckled.

"Don't laugh. These 'abductions,' as you called them, are starting to bug me."

"Oh, come on, Joe! You letting those senile old farts get to you? You know they're either exaggerating, or they're a little bit off in the head. You can't take those guys seriously."

"I realize that," Donnelly said. "But then why have there been so many reportings recently? Are *all* those guys crazy?"

"I don't know…I just know you, and I know you're going to get all wrapped up in this mess until you can't find your way out. You take things way too seriously, man, that's your problem. You gotta relax more, stop thinking so much."

"I know," Donnelly said. "I was just thinking though…"

"There you go again, man. Let it go. It'll work itself out." Gregory drained the last of his beer.

Donnelly stared at his friend, lips pursed, determined. "You know what I did this afternoon? I drove by all four of the locations where the homeless men were reported missing—"

"Joe…"

"—and I searched the areas off the interstate for any clues, anything unusual that might have been overlooked." Pause. "Nothing. Not a damn thing. But you know what I *did* notice?"

"What?" Gregory asked.

"Kudzu."

"Huh?"

"Kudzu, man. There's fuckin' kudzu vines creeping and crawling all over the place out there. It's like that green shit has overrun everything—the ground, the concrete embankment, the hills, the entire forest! When did that happen? And have you seen how it configures itself into animals and people and stuff when it climbs up and down trees and poles? I used to think it looked cool when I was a kid. Now, it just freaks me out. I really don't like the vibe I'm getting from it."

"Damn, Joe, would you listen to yourself? I can't believe I'm hearing this from you! You gotta take it easy, man, gain some perspective. Trust me."

Donnelly sighed wearily. "I guess so…it's just that something about the scenes wasn't right and I don't know what it is. I don't know how else to put it."

"Well, when you find out what it is, you let me know. Until then, let's get another round."

"My turn," Donnelly said, forcing a grin on his face.

⌐

A couple days later the City Slasher struck again, same MO, practically the same everything, only this time the victim was discovered off of Summer Avenue and White Station, several miles east of the previous murder and even further removed from the city proper. Gregory puzzled momentarily over this recent development, but quickly put it on the back burner in favor of the one bit of good news they had uncovered from the crime scene: they had a witness! He'd finally caught a break.

A grizzled, middle-aged, white homeless man, who just happened to be trudging down White Station around 4:30 that morning due to his purported "insomnier," claimed to have observed a moderately tall and thin white male, somewhere between the ages of thirty and forty-five, wearing a dark, lightweight hoodie and carrying a glistening metal object, fleeing north up Summer Avenue away from the bloody crime scene. Within the hour Gregory corralled the department's sketch artist and, with information elicited from their lone witness, a rough composite of the City Slasher was drafted. By mid-morning the four major TV news stations and the *Commercial Appeal* had been provided with a drawing of the suspected killer for airing and for use in the print media. In addition, patrol officers had been armed with copies of the sketch and tasked to canvass their respective neighborhoods during the course of their work day in an effort to drum up any new leads on the suspected killer's whereabouts.

All in all, Gregory thought, despite the tragic loss of yet another life, he believed he'd finally turned the corner in his investigation.

⤿

Two days later, Donnelly had just arrived at work downtown for his regular morning shift when he noticed that an Incident Report had been dropped off on his desk. Scanning the handwritten document, he realized that, to his chagrin, another homeless man had been reported missing in the county late last night. And judging by the wording in the narrative, the deputy who had taken the statement didn't put much credence in the complainant's story, and had never even notified Donnelly of this recent news. Donnelly wondered if that blasé feeling was slowly infecting the rest of his department like a disease. After all, the complainants weren't reputable individuals by any stretch of the imagination, so he couldn't blame his peers and subordinates if they shared the deputy's sentiment. Nevertheless, clutching the paperwork, he retrieved his suit coat and left the squad bullpen, determined to check out the scene of this latest "abduction," as his buddy had kiddingly phrased it.

Donnelly edged his cruiser off the road and into the breakdown lane in the vicinity of mile marker 23 on I-40 West. Climbing carefully out of his vehicle as interstate traffic barreled by him at seventy miles an hour, he mentally rehashed his conversation with Russell the other night, smiling over how ecstatic his buddy had been after the big break in his case. He'd said they were now fielding scores of leads every day, and it was just a matter of time 'til one of them panned out and the killer was apprehended.

As Donnelly cautiously made his way over to the Chambers Chapel Road overpass, beneath which the latest derelict had gone missing, the fact that this location was even closer to the city wasn't lost on him. It was like some sort of insidious pattern or trend. *What the hell is going on*? he wondered.

Upon reaching the sloping concrete base under the overpass, Donnelly methodically scoured the entire area, hoping to find a clue or an overlooked piece of evidence that would shed some light on these highly enigmatic disappearances. But other than trace amounts of litter and debris, which the wind from interstate traffic pushed to and fro like a yo-yo, there was nothing of substance to catalogue or report. However, as before, there was still the over-whelming presence of the kudzu.

Damn, he thought, *it's all over the place!*

He moved closer to the steep embankment, subtly improving his vantage point.

The weed-like green vine had crept more than ten feet onto the canted concrete slab from either direction, effectively carpeting and camouflaging a sizeable portion of the transients' temporary haven. It was mind-boggling how hardy and pervasive the vine could be. With his attention focused on the center of the sloping area and his mind running in circles, an almost imperceptible motion to the right drew his head around.

What the hell was that? he thought, his brow furrowed in concentration.

Musta been the wind or my imagination, he rationalized, staring intently at the spot where a moment ago he could've sworn he'd seen something. But there was nothing out of the ordinary and nothing more happened.

Until he turned to go.

A couple tentacle-like strands of the kudzu stretched their lengths along the pavement as if they were just waking up, inching in his direction with a barely audible scratching sound.

"What the fuck?!" he cried, jumping backwards a few feet.

Sweat now trickling down his forehead from more than just the summer heat, he gazed once again at the spot where he had just seen activity in the vines. But after a long minute with no repeat performance, he breathed a sigh of relief and chalked it up to his vivid imagination and preoccupation with this ongoing mystery.

Retracing the path to his vehicle on shaky legs, he questioned whether or not he was being honest with himself.

Late that evening, well after his shift was over, Donnelly steeled himself against his enduring irrational apprehension and returned to the various I-40 West overpasses, to conduct a cursory drive-by of the locations. Aside from a couple of homeless men setting up camp for the night beneath one particular overpass, however, he noticed nothing unusual. *Probably too early*, he guessed, and decided to return a little later the following evening.

⤺

Over the next several nights, Donnelly repeated his spot checks of the areas of blight, as he thought of them both literally and figuratively, generally cruising down the interstate around 3:00 or 4:00 in the morning. But, for the time being, his efforts proved to be fruitless.

⤺

A week after Gregory had caught a break in the City Slasher case, he and Donnelly met up at their customary restaurant/bar to talk and bring each other up to speed.

"Still 'all quiet on the western front?'" Donnelly said with a smile after their pitcher of beer had arrived.

"Shit," Gregory said, pouring himself a glass. "I guess no news is good news…The guy must be layin' low for the time being. I mean, we've saturated the downtown area with extra patrols, distributed hundreds of flyers, and the TV news stations have covered the story every few days. He must be scared to come out of hiding now."

"That sounds good," Donnelly said, helping himself to a glass. "Maybe he'll stay that way."

"Nah, I don't think so, man," Gregory said. "He's going to kill again, for sure. I just hope we catch him before that happens."

"Yeah, I suppose you're right," Donnelly said, sipping at his beer, lost in thought. "Kinda weird, huh, how both your killer and my 'abductor' have quieted down at the same time? I know I had that one disappearance a day or so after your Slasher struck, but for the better part of a week, nothing."

"Joe," Gregory said, putting down his mug. "I'm not trying to make light of your investigation or anything, but those missing old men aren't victims of some strange conspiracy or mass kidnapping. They just walked off, or maybe the guys who told you they were abducted are crazy. You watch, when this is all said and done, you'll see I'm right. Mark my words."

"I'm listening, man, but I just have this feeling there's more to it than that." Donnelly paused, hands rubbing the condensation off his glass. "You know, for the past five or six nights, I've been doing these early-morning drive-bys at all of the locations on the interstate where those guys were reported missing. Maybe I'm obsessed—so sue me! It's my nature, you already know that. I just can't let it go. And last week, I was under the Chambers Chapel Road overpass, checking it out in the middle of the morning, when I saw—"

"What'd you see?" Gregory said, raising his eyebrows.

Donnelly was glad he'd caught himself. He couldn't let his friend hear what he *thought* he'd seen that day. The vines moving. After all, it had simply been his imagination, right? Besides, if Russell thought he was going off the deep end over this one case he would probably make the call to Lakeside Mental Hospital himself. It's what he'd do if the situation were reversed.

"Ahhh, nothing. I don't know what I was thinking about. It was nothing."

Gregory eyeballed him doubtfully for a moment, then said, "Ohh-kay...Uhh, you all right, Joe?"

"Yeah, I'm fine. Come on," Donnelly said, picking up the pitcher and refilling their glasses, "have another drink."

The subject dropped, they clinked glasses in a toast and chatted for another couple of hours.

↬

The following night, more out of habit than a sense of duty, Donnelly once again found himself travelling west on I-40 around 3:30 in the morning. All appeared quiet until he approached mile marker 20, the Canada Road exit.

"What's going on over there?" he whispered to himself.

From a couple hundred yards away, he was just able to discern some type of commotion occurring beneath the overpass. As the distance narrowed, the dim light afforded by headlights of east- and westbound traffic allowed him to see that a ballet-like struggle was going on between two or more individuals. Easing his foot off the gas pedal, he cautiously pulled off the interstate into the breakdown lane, coasting to a stop about a hundred yards short of where the altercation was taking place. He quickly killed the lights, shut off the engine, and, in lieu of slapping the blue light atop the roof of his vehicle and alerting the combatants, settled for flicking on his hazard lights to warn westbound traffic of his presence. Grabbing his trusty Maglite and ensuring that he was strapped, he edged quietly out of his car and softly closed the door with a muffled *thwack*.

Hurriedly creeping forward on the inside of the breakdown lane, Donnelly drew his Sig Sauer P229 semi-automatic pistol from his holster with his right hand, and fumbled with the flashlight with his left. Tunnel vision kicking in, adrenaline pumping, he swore he could hear his own labored breathing above the relentless din of traffic. "Damn...you're...out of shape...Joe," he said to himself, as he closed on the scene.

When he finally veered, out of breath as a life-long smoker, around the closest foundation abutment and reached the base of the sloped embankment, he flicked his Maglite on and targeted it at the embankment's uppermost portion, bringing his weapon to bear as well. "Freeze!" he shouted. "Stop right now!"

Pinned by his beam like a deer in headlights was a tall, youngish white male, wearing a dark hoodie, and brandishing a large hunting knife whose serrated edge was coated with blood.

Oh, my God! he thought, realizing that no more than thirty or forty feet separated him from the City Slasher. The killer had been lying low for a while now, Donnelly knew, and he had practically forgotten all about him. But with the full-court press the Memphis Police Department had been applying recently, apparently the Slasher had no alternative but to continue his killing spree out east in the county, away from the city.

Tearing himself from the myriad thoughts crowding his mind,

Donnelly fought his tunnel vision and brought his focus back to the scene at hand.

The killer standing before him.

And the profusely bleeding individual lying not twenty feet to his side.

"Don't move, d'you hear me?" Donnelly cried, scrambling unsteadily up the sloping embankment with his gun and one eye trained on the Slasher, his other eye on the still, rag-doll body closer to him.

When he reached the prone man, he dropped to his knees, his pants legs instantly soaking in blood. He clumsily socked the Maglite under his right armpit and directed the beam and his weapon at the killer, while blindly feeling for the victim's wounds with his other hand.

"Stay right there you sonofabitch!" he said before discovering the long, wet, ragged slash to the elderly man's throat. Blood was everywhere, he realized, and had even sprayed across the poor man's chest to pool in his crotch. Thick rivulets had also spilled from the deep, mortal wound like a burst dam and tracked lazily down the concrete's sloped surface. Its coppery tang hung in the air like a mist. Donnelly found it impossible to try for a pulse at the man's ruined neck, and he became even more disheartened when he was unable to find one after grasping one of the man's wrists for several seconds.

He stood slowly, unconsciously wiping his blood-coated hand on his stained slacks as he faced the nameless killer.

"Drop the fucking knife!" he shouted, transferring the flashlight back to his free hand. "Do it! *Now!*"

The hooded killer chuckled, wagging the tainted knife. "I don't think so," he said.

Donnelly stepped closer to the murderer, rage radiating off him in waves. "I said, *drop the fucking knife!*"

But even before the Slasher could respond, a flood of kudzu surged toward him like a tidal wave, the vines wrapping around his legs from behind, crawling and climbing up his body, reaching for and encircling his neck, then dragging him to the ground. The crimson-splattered knife in his hand clattered harmlessly to the pavement.

Holy shit! Donnelly thought, stumbling backwards several feet. He'd been right after all. The fucking kudzu was alive! Standing there in shock, he giggled maniacally and holstered his weapon. He wondered what Russell would say when he heard about this.

As the carnivorous vines squeezed tighter around the killer, choking off the man's muffled cries and strangling him, pulsing with unbelievable sentient life, they slowly and methodically pulled him off the concrete slab and into the tangled chaos of their carpet-like core. Alternately flexing and relaxing, the kudzu quickly began digesting the helpless victim, as it had done so many times before with other unfortunate men. Donnelly wondered if nature was striking back in retaliation for all the horrors mankind had wreaked upon it over the decades. Was this confined to Memphis alone? Or was it happening elsewhere, as well? The world perhaps? A natural storm, with nature trying to reclaim what was rightfully hers from the very beginning. God, he hoped not.

He realized he needed to call this in. But the deceased derelict wasn't going anywhere, and he didn't want the City Slasher going anywhere ever again. *Just a couple more minutes,* he thought. Both he and Russell needed closure in their investigations. Although, in his case, lengthy study and research would undoubtedly follow.

After a few more minutes he caught the faint sound of sirens in the distance. Passersby must have called 911 to alert law enforcement to what was happening at his location, he guessed. *Ah, well,* he thought, *it's time.*

He bent over and carefully picked up the bloody hunting knife with his handkerchief. Russell would need it for forensic evidence to make his case, he knew. Then he walked back along the interstate to his cruiser. Placing the flashlight and evidence on the front passenger-side floorboard, he pulled out his cell phone, flipped it open, and punched in his friend's number.

A SMALL SAND STORM

KEN GOLDMAN

Ken Goldman, an affiliate member of the Horror Writers Association, has homes on the Main Line in Pennsylvania and at the Jersey shore, depending upon his mood and the track of the sun. His stories appear in over 600 independent press publications in the US, Canada, the UK, and Australia, with over twenty published in 2010. Since 1993 his tales have received seven honorable mentions in *The Year's Best Fantasy & Horror* anthologies. His book of short stories, *You Had Me At ARRGH!!: Five Uneasy Pieces by Ken Goldman* (Sam's Dot Publishers), had been an all-time top ten bestseller at the former Genre Mall from 2007–2011, and his novella *Desiree* is available in ebook downloadable format on the Damnation Books website, and on Amazon in Kindle and print format. You may find Ken on the websites Masters of Horror and The Horror Cafe.

I'M SMARTER THAN MOST PEOPLE. YES, IT SOUNDS AR-rogant, I know that. But it's what my father taught me, and for the most part I've found it to be true. As Dad would say, some are born smart and some are born strong because that's Nature's method of balancing her scales. One look at my father's toothpick frame and you knew he must have been among those born smart. Cancer sent him to his grave last winter, but during his eighty-three years never once did he raise his fists in anger, not even in self-defense. My dad didn't have to. Never had to run away from a fight neither, just in case you were wondering. The man was too intelligent to forfeit a tooth over some ridiculous issue that next day probably wouldn't mean a bug fart to him. He could use his wits to talk some slap-happy jerk out of practically anything that perturbed him. My dad, he taught me to always take the high road and walk away. It wasn't much of a talent to leave his only son, but it's one that has served me well.

Okay, so maybe you're thinking even Jesus sometimes had to take it on the chin, and some might call my backing off from physical confrontation ill-becoming behavior for any male hoping to call himself a man. Me, I consider it plain common sense, and until recently I had managed to keep my teeth intact, along with most of my dignity. And we all know what happened to Jesus.

Anyway, I wanted to tell you this so you would understand that what occurred that day on the beach wasn't my fault. Maybe it was nobody's fault. People are what they are and that's why they do what they do, and sometimes during the everyday act of getting on with your life two dissimilar personality types manage to collide. The world isn't big enough to avoid it.

I know I've never looked the type to share a beach with tanned Adonis sorts who probably shit bigger than I stand. For one thing, being fair-skinned and thin, I don't tan in the sun so much as stroke. I tend to turn pink and fry like a strip of bacon. Most swim trunks slide down my waist because I don't really have one to hold them up. And my hair never looked good windblown, especially now that I have so little of it. Some woman once told me I looked like I had a wind sock blowing from my scalp. But I can tolerate all that without much humiliation. You see, I've always liked being near the surf, so I don't give a damn about appearances. To be truthful no one much notices me anyway.

Of course, my social invisibility would never likely send an attractive woman's gaze in my direction. Not an unattractive one's either, for that matter. Honestly, most women don't even remember my name, and when they happen to recollect it, it's always just plain Stanley, my given name—not Stan or Stanton, even if I tell them I'd prefer one of these others. I suppose that must mean something, but I'm not sure what. There are advantages to seeming invisible, though. I don't enjoy talking to strangers much. See, making conversation isn't one of my stronger points either. So, that's me, Stanley Walters, the strong silent type, if you scratch the "strong" part. Go ahead and laugh if you have to. I'm okay with it. Really.

Anyway, that day on the beach, what I first notice is the girl's scream. At first I think maybe she's in some kind of trouble. But, no, it isn't anything like that.

"Eeeeeeeee!!!!"

That's how it all begins, with that simple exclamation of sheer summertime joy that comes so often from the mouths of nubile young women in bikinis. The girl is splashing around in the ocean with some muscle-bound ape, her boyfriend probably, the type who seems he was born pumping iron—that tanned sinewy sort who's capable of attracting the pick of the beach bunny litter without even half trying. The guy keeps disappearing beneath the waves like some amusement park dolphin, then popping up just where his dark-haired young beauty stands, each of them bobbing up and down wrapped around each other in that rolling surf. Sometimes he lifts her high on his shoulders, then drops her, laughing, into the water, only to retrieve her and do it again. I doubt if during my entire life I've experienced a moment of such unrestrained exuberance, and often I wonder what that sensation must feel like. Inside my head I picture myself hoisting a pretty girl on my shoulders without giving myself a hernia, listening to her shriek with glee like some damsel in distress awaiting my rescue.

["Eeeeeee…"]

Yeah, right. It makes me feel vaguely ridiculous just thinking it. Supporting any kind of weight on my shoulders would probably make me fold up like my beach chair. Besides, some people aren't cut out for an uninhibited approach to life, and that sort of unbridled laughter would just stick in my throat like a chicken bone. There's a certain injustice to it, I suppose, but no one said life had to be fair. Well, who am I to complain? It isn't as if I'm blind or in a wheelchair, for Christ's sake.

So there I am sitting on the beach finding it impossible to concentrate on the *Times* article on why American liberalism is dead, because all I can think about is that damned couple having one hell of a good time in the Atlantic and whether that girl's bikini might fly off with the next breaker. I'm watching them when suddenly I don't see the girl there any more. The gorilla is in the water all right, and he's laughing himself hoarse like the jackass I have no doubt he is, and I notice he's pressing down on the top of that girl's head, holding her under the water like it's the most clever thing in the world. She's struggling to breathe, and every now and then he allows her head to pop up so she can get some air into her lungs. Then he's pushing her down again, and *(Ha! Ha!)* isn't that the funniest thing you ever saw, hey? Let's do it again! And again!

Well, somehow she manages to break herself free from this Neanderthal, and she's angry; you can see how angry she is. But the beefy boyfriend, he's still laughing even while she makes her way back to shore without even looking behind, she's so irate. She storms right past me to their blanket and begins packing her things into a huge straw bag, throwing suntan lotion and glasses and a yellow Frisbee into that bag like she can't get off the beach fast enough. I look back towards the surf and the ape man is sloshing his way out of the water to catch up with her, no doubt to talk some of his version of reason into her.

"Stop acting like a cunt! I was only kidding around!"

"I almost drowned! You're a fucking jerk!"

He reaches for the bag. She pulls it close to her and tries to walk away. He grabs her, shakes her.

"You're not going anywhere!"

"Leave me alone!"

All right, so I'm thinking this is none of my business, even though I'm sitting not fifteen paces from this little drama. Keeping my nose clean has kept it from being broken, and I have no intentions of altering that philosophy now. Except...

...except he's shaking her, shaking her really hard.

"Stop it, cunt! Stop it right now, goddammit!"

"Let go of me!"

He drags her back to the blanket, not giving a shit that everything inside her beach bag drops out as he hauls her. But she isn't going easily, digging her feet into the sand and swinging her arms at him every step of the way. That just makes the gorilla tug her harder. When they get to the blanket he pushes her down, and we're not talking about friendly persuasion here.

"Cunt!"

"Jerk!"

Maybe I forget for a moment that this is all happening in real time and isn't some idiot afternoon soaper on TV. I don't really know what's going on inside my head except that I'm drawn in by the theatrics of it. In any case, I can't take my eyes from what is transpiring in front of me. I might be smirking a little bit, I don't know. If I am, that must be what catches this goon's attention and sets him off.

"Hey!" He stops his harassment of the girl and looks at me. His eyes set a bead like some predatory animal. *"Yeah, you, you bald prick! Do you find this amusing?"* I look away, try burying my face behind the *Times*. But he isn't buying it. *"Hey fuckstick! I'm talking to you!"*

I consider packing up my chair and belongings right then and there, and heading for safer territory. But it's too late for that. Kong is coming over. The girl's voice now reveals none of the anger of the past few minutes. Now she sounds frightened.

"Eddie...don't..."

But this Eddie, he doesn't seem to hear his woman speaking to him. Towering over me stands a man with a plan.

"You enjoying this, are you? How about I wipe that smile off your ugly face?"

Remaining silent no longer seems an option, but even *I* hear the trepidation in my own voice.

"Listen, I didn't—"

"Get up! Get out of that fucking chair!"

His words sound slurred, like maybe he had enjoyed a little liquid encouragement before his trip to the beach. And seeing the guy close up is a completely different experience. He isn't exactly smiling, but there in the corner of his mouth I can see a hole where a tooth should have been. I can only guess how he might have lost that molar but I have a pretty good idea. He wears a tattoo high on his muscled arm, a bleeding heart with a jagged-edged dagger piercing through it. This does not bode well.

What would Dad do...? Oh Jesus, what would Dad do...?

[I'm smarter than most people...I'm smarter than most people...]

Big Eddie, he doesn't wait for me to get to my feet. He pulls me from my chair, shakes me like he had shaken his bikini-clad companion moments earlier.

"Not smiling now, are you, cocksuck?"

The girl vaults from their blanket.

"Eddie, damn it! Stop it! Stop it now!" She pulls at him, but he doesn't loosen his grasp one bit. Words aren't coming easily while he shakes me, but I manage a few.

"Listen, you don't have to do this—"

"Shudda fugg up!!!"

I don't know if the bruiser means me or the girl, but it doesn't matter. He tosses me ass first into the sand like I'm last week's dirty laundry. To make sure I get his point he kicks me right in the head, mashing my face into the sand with his foot. His heel strikes my jaw so hard I think I hear my teeth rattle, and for a moment I'm pretty certain I talked to God. Sure enough my swim trunks slide half-way down my ass, and I tug them up fast because on the flip side I'm showing a bit of my religion.

The girl is now pleading.

"That's enough, Eddie! That's enough, okay?"

And for Eddie, I guess it is. He leaves me there.

I should mention that we aren't entirely alone on the beach. There are other people around, some even with kids, and everyone within earshot watched this whole scene unravel. But no one made a move to intervene, no good Samaritan stepped forward to protest this troglodyte's unseemly beach behavior in front of their kids. And someone, some young girl, I think it was, she even giggled when I hit the sand. That giggle hurt more than the beefer's intimidation.

Now I'll admit I've had moments of humiliation during my life. But this experience shot right to the top of the list. I'm lying there with sand in my mouth commingling with blood because during all this I must have bitten my tongue pretty good and it's making this grainy paste that's dribbling down my chin. I'm crumpled in the sand not knowing whether to get to my feet and receive more pain for my effort, or just keep lying there until high tide. Regardless of my decision I have already become the afternoon's laughingstock to anyone around me—a timid excuse for a man, whose disgrace will provide a light moment of conversation during tonight's barbecue.

When I manage to make that long trip back to my beach chair it seems the sunbathing world has returned to normal, with kids screaming while their parents yammer. In fact Kong and his bikinied beach trophy are on their blanket kissing away like none of this ever happened, while I'm still tasting crunchy blood on my tongue. To all around me I have returned to the Land of the Invisible, and at that moment I would have felt no surprise had my own shadow no longer been there.

I know better than to stare at the passion play taking place on that blanket. But then I notice something glimmering in the sand not far from where the orangutan lies practically on top of his playmate. Some object has fallen from the girl's beach bag during the lovers' melee and has gone unnoticed during their recapturing of the scattered items. I'm thinking, *Okay, sleeping dogs are lying, let them lay or hump or whatever it is those two are doing.* There seems no need to go another round with this maniac. But then Dad comes to mind, and he refuses to remain silent.

The high road, son...take the high road...

Okay, I'm thinking, *I can be big about this, I can rise above all the horseshit and also be smart, even though this psychopathic cowboy has just shaken the snot out of me.* It appears that's the girl's iPod half buried there in the sand, and the right thing to do would be just to pick that sucker up and return it to her to show that doofus, see? This Stan Walters, he knows how to take it like a man, and how do you like those particular apples, Tarzan? While those two are making out like ferrets in heat they don't even notice me as I pick that gizmo out of the sand and wipe it off right in front of them. For a moment I'm thinking, *Hell, maybe I should just pocket the iPod and consider it compensation for the ordeal that asshole has put me through*. But Dad wouldn't have liked that. So standing over them, I clear my throat…

"Excuse me…" I say it only once, but loud.

The two look up, and for several god-awful seconds no one says anything because that moment seems too damned bizarre to be real. I speak first.

"You dropped this in the sand, see…" I say, holding out the iPod to the girl. Ol' Eddie looks at me as if I'm handing his woman a steaming turd. She takes it but says nothing, probably too star-tled—or maybe embarrassed—to know *what* to say. But Edward, he suddenly finds a voice. He turns to his girl.

"Yours?"

"Not mine," she says. "I don't own an iPod. Look, the name on it says 'Kenny.'"

Kong looks up at me. "Thanks, chief. Gloria here says it's not hers. But we'll keep it anyway, if that's all right with you."

[…the high road…the high road…]

So I say, "It's not all right with me. That belongs to someone, maybe some little kid. I'll hand it over to the lifeguard." I hold my hand out for it, already knowing what to expect.

The girl makes a gesture to hand the iPod back to me, but her Eddie isn't having any of that. He stops her, holds Gloria's arm.

"I don't think so, sport."

Some little voice inside me is warning, *Leave this alone, Stanley, walk away right now, he's holding all the cards and you've got noth-ing, so walk away and keep your teeth for another day…*

I don't listen to that little voice. My rage finds a voice of its own.

"That isn't right. You know it isn't right, you fucking ape!"

Eddie looks at me as if I had just cornholed his grandmother. For a moment he seems amused, but that expression melts fast. The horror returns to Gloria's eyes, that "Shit, here-we-go-again" look I had seen earlier.

"Eddie, no…" she manages to say, but he's already on his feet.

"You didn't learn a whole lot the last time, did you, fuckstick?"

But ol' Eddie, he's wrong about that. I had learned plenty.

Now, I've already told you that I'm smarter than most people. I don't know much about fighting, but I know a little about self-defense just from watching the Information Channel. Like, did you know that if you use the bottom of your palm and give a good upward thrust to your opponent's nose you'll drive cartilage from the nose directly into his brain, causing immediate death if you do it quickly enough? Well, I'm betting that Eddie doesn't know that. But I don't take the time to ask him. I just act the minute that palooka gets to his feet. Don't even give him the chance to throw his first punch. *Ka-pow!* and yippee-kay-yay, motherfucker!

His hands go to his nose, and for a moment I think he smiles, probably with visions of my imminent death dancing in his head. But then his lights go out, and he topples face forward into the sand like a felled tree. And that's all she wrote, folks.

Yeah, there are cheers from someone nearby, but not from his Gloria, that's damned sure. She sees there is more damage done than simply a lucky knockout punch. The woman kneels gasping over her fallen giant, seeming unable to comprehend the moment. Then she glares at me.

"Jesus, what have you done?"

It seems pretty clear to me what I've done.

Some guy in the crowd runs over, holds Eddie's eyelid open, and sees the orb roll back like a doll's. "I think…I think he's dead…" the man says.

A few gasps escape from the onlookers, and already I'm considering the consequences. I turn to the circle of people surrounding us. "You all saw what he did to me, right? I mean, I had to…You all saw that I had to, didn't you? That man was going to kill me!" I turn to Gloria. "He *was* going to kill me," I repeat.

Gloria just looks at me.

⤳

Oddly enough, she didn't disagree. In fact, Gloria didn't say anything. Because, as I discovered later, slap-happy Eddie once *had* killed some guy a few years earlier in an idiot barroom brawl. It was accidental with no intent to kill, as his lawyer had convinced the jurors, and that fracas explained the missing tooth that Eddie in subsequent years had considered some kind of badge of honor, telling his story to anyone who would listen. None of which did that shit sack's case any good when Gloria explained all that to the judge who was considering my circumstances months later. Judge Ernest T. Gracey took a long look at me, spent a few minutes studying the rap sheet of Mr. Edward DiBaccio, and made his decision before lunchtime. The whole thing never even went to trial.

Dismissed. Over. The end.

You would think so, wouldn't you?

But like I mentioned, I'm smarter than most people, so I'll tell you right now that no, that wasn't the end. Not by a long shot. Because I'm the kind of guy who learns not to make the same mistake twice. And what happened that day on the beach, well, that wasn't exactly a mistake. Oh, I didn't intend it to happen in front of so many witnesses because it gets messy when others are involved. I would have preferred to walk away, but Eddie changed the rules and I did what I had to do when I sent his nose slamming into his frontal lobe. Because what I intended to do wasn't supposed to happen until later, when I planned to follow him and find him alone.

Of course, no one thought to look inside my car, so no one knew what my true intentions were that day—what my intentions always are when it comes to denizens like Mr. Eddie DiBaccio. They're everywhere, those fucking predators, and Dad always told me someone ought to thin their stinking herd because Nature's scales always needed balancing. There will be others like Eddie, of course, just like there were others before him. I guess guys like me just set them off. But Eddie, he was the first with whom I had to go mano a mano to get the job done.

See, most times I use this ice pick…

tornado brewing

CAROL ALEXANDER

Carol Alexander is a writer and editor for trade and educational publishing, and the author of numerous children's books. In 2011–2012, her work appeared in *Avocet*, *Cave Moon Press*, *Chiron Review*, *The Canary*, *Danse Macabre*, *Earthspeak*, *Fade*, *Mobius*, *Numinous*, *OVS Magazine*, and other print and online journals.

Across the ragged field we came, sweaters tied around our waists,
cat-calling as ringlets frizzed and static fashioned webs of those fine hairs
edging the temples and the pulsing brow, tender blue veins of children,
wide lumen of the heart's blood traveling in its slow, circuitous way.

Clouds of dark-eyed juncos skimmed the wicked crest of sky
towering up above the fields, fields of ripe September crackling
under foot, locusts and crawling beetles battling through dry corn.
We laughed about the cellars, taunts flung to the whipping clouds.

They warned us of the season, those guardians of the central plain:
but we were careless of their words until the flailing funnel spread
its reechy fingers for our skirts, our whirling shocks of hair—
here was the beast, brewed in devil's cauldron, warmed and stirred

then beaten to its final fearsome shape, throwing shadows down,
blackening the stalky, stubbled fields, corn knives stabbing at our legs.
Then indeed we ran ourselves to ground, bursting lungs in flame,
and reached the cellar door, words of praise babbling in the turgid air.

BUBBLE

PETER GOODWIN

Peter D. Goodwin divides his time between the streets and vibrant clutter of New York City and the remnants of the natural world along Maryland's Chesapeake Bay. Peter has had poems published in the anthologies *September Eleven: Maryland Voices*, *Listening to Water: The Susquehanna Watershed Anthology*, *Alternatives To Surrender*, and *Wild Things: Domestic and Otherwise*, as well as in various journals including *Rattle*, *Memoir (and)*, *River Poets Journal*, *Delaware Poetry Review*, *Yellow Medicine Review*, *Twisted Tongue*, *Poetry Monthly*, *Main Street Rag*, and *Anon*.

Long legs stretched across
the aisle of a city bus
suede boots
high-heeled suede boots
high-heeled, stiletto-heeled suede boots
tight jeans
jeans sculptured to sheath young tight bodies
luxurious lines of their knit blouses
they could be graceful if they wanted
they are anything they want
two beautiful bodies bent
leaning towards each other
their long locks intertwining
sharing iPod plugs
sharing music, sharing intimacies
tapping on their cell phones
oblivious to the rattle, the rumble of the bus
the scratchy intonations from the driver
the low mumble of other conversations
their long legs stretched across the aisle
oblivious to other people
stepping over their stretched legs
oblivious to the world
oblivious to the darkening sky
oblivious to the dirty rain that will wash
the pride from their boots
those precious prideful stiletto-heeled suede boots
believing the weather will always be fair
their future as wonderful as their now
that others will always admire their youth and beauty
content to step over their stretched legs
indifferent to the silences and glances of others
indifferent to whatever is beyond their horizon
unaware that the present will soon be past
unaware, indifferent to that bubble on the horizon
that storm which will wash away their world
ruin their stiletto-heeled suede boots
scattering their illusions
bursting their bubble.

MEMOIR: THE STORM
OF THE CENTURY

LESLIE SILTON

Leslie is a book editor and writer's coach who started life as a poet, with stops along the way in acting, folk music, art classes in Paris, and a BFA at the Massachusetts College of Art. She has published six chapbooks and been published in various poetry anthologies and online, as well as recorded on CDs and live on the radio. She has participated in over 150 open mics in Boston, NYC, Los Angeles, and Paris, France, and has exhibited and sold paintings and photographs. Leslie is now the facilitator of a writing workshop running twice a month since 1991 and has performed at Mt. Holyoke College and MIT. Even though Leslie's career includes a children's play performed at Theatre-on-the-Wharf in Boston, a student ballet at Antioch College based on a prose poem, art workshops at Red Cross shelters for earthquake victims in Los Angeles, and two murals painted to promote Human Rights, writing has become her main creative outlet. In addition to a short story published on the web in June 2012 and a new online magazine selecting a poem for publication, she has completed a dozen other short stories, three novellas, and two novels. Her magnum opus may turn out to be the fantasy story she's been working on for nearly a decade. She'd like to give a nod to her fantastic brothers, Michael and Bruce, who are both first-class artists and writers. Looks like art just runs in the family.

DAY ONE

Through the window I could see that snow was falling again with a kind of anthropomorphic energy.

Aww. That's just showing off. Go away, I thought. But the wind did seem to have hands, because the glass panes were being rattled. *Maybe there is going to be a storm after all.*

Outside, the temperature was hovering just above freezing, just high enough to permit snow flurries. But the cold weather wasn't going to mess with me. Blasts of heat from my antique radiator permitted me to leave my wool scarf untied while in the apartment.

On and off all day long, the wind was noisy and surging but I ignored it because I felt safe in my solid old brick building. Of course the radio and television news were suggesting we might be in for a storm. *But hey,* I thought, *you can't scare us.* Some winter days the wind chill factor in Boston brings the temperature down to a revolting 40 below. Big fat deal. Anyway, the Red Cross was across the street from my building in case being air-lifted was someone's choice-of-rescue dream.

When I went to the store that morning, it looked like everyone in the city had shopped for the kind of food that doesn't require anything more than a can opener, two slices of bread, or liquid reconstitution. Extra batteries and candles had been practically inhaled by the buying public. I'll bet I wasn't the only one with bottled water lining the kitchen counters.

So there's a storm coming, I thought. *We can handle it.* The TV kept providing weather report updates, like an Election Day countdown. What's a few days off because it snowed?

It had been a decade since we'd had a winter storm of magnitude. Even situated, annoyingly, in the path of the very unsubtle Montreal Express, no one really believed that anything meteorological was actually going to cause us any real inconvenience. It was the old "cry wolf."

Later on, after all hell had broken loose, we finally admitted we hadn't grasped the situation—after Mother Nature had toyed with us long enough, she unleashed the full measure of her dreadful weight and fury. How then the bitter cold sat on us like a massive anvil as we heard the ringing of the final hammer of deepest winter beating us, the people, into thin strips of tin who moved only with great effort, by piercing the air, one footstep at a time.

But that was still the future, and right now my class assignment sat in front of me on my easel and it wanted completion. *That* was serious business. I could forget about some stupid old storm.

The personal iconography I had been developing had so far been refused recognition by my instructors. I felt like certain ways of looking at the world were being pushed on me. What was that about? I mean, what's supposed to happen anyway when the imagination of an artist gets fired up? Are we supposed to wear blinders like horses?

I read art history.

This year I've been sitting in darkened rooms while a very dull man showed us hundreds of colored slides—starting with the caves of France. I'd already read the letters of Gauguin and Van Gogh, and they weren't class assignments. I'd been to museums in six countries and attended numerous exhibitions. I knew something about art.

I think the three painting instructors at my previous Review were *starting* to "get" what I was doing, they just didn't want to admit it. They couldn't believe their own emotional responses.

One of them actually said, "Why do I get a good feeling from that?"

My answer was, "Because that's what I meant for the painting to do."

But the jerk just shook his head. "Oh no. I'm not that easily affected." And then he got all weird on me. "*Why* did you paint it that way? What were you thinking of? Are you sure about that passage there?"

I could hardly stand it anymore. What kind of art school...in fact, what kind of a world was this anyway? They didn't want to teach. They just wanted to pontificate.

I put the water on to boil. Time for some tea. Sitting in my little kitchen nook, I felt very stirred up. It turned out I'd been practically holding my breath. So, I took a deep breath and calmed down. I was ready to go back to work.

DAY TWO

I finished the painting.

Outside my window the sky was going black even though it was still mid-afternoon. The wind was actually howling. Snow was falling. But not just any snow. A hard snow. Shades of Bob Dylan and his "Hard Rain."

Being tucked into my big chair with a couple of blankets provided me with some comfort and solace. Hearing the heat rattle and knock inside the radiator protectively, I felt less threatened by the cold pressing at me. It was getting nasty outside beyond the old panes of glass but I had things to think about.

Turning on the radio I heard our local meteorologists getting positively giddy over the prospects of negotiating us through the coming storm. Boy, do news people love trouble. The coming storm was apparently a financial bonanza as their audience tuned in and the Speedy Gonzales announcer doubled up on the quickie ads.

I decided I should be worrying about my next painting. *Oh, those weathercasters. They get so dramatic*, I thought. Such serious expressions as they began massing the magnetized snow cloud pieces on the TV map.

On the other hand, it did look as though the storm had gathered shape. That was interesting to me, as an artist. But I also noticed that the intensity of the wind had increased dramatically so I dialed up my school. After six or seven rings the phone was picked up. A man answered.

"Everything is closed," he said. "Stay inside."

I had an instant of fear in case he was wrong. I would be marked absent for having been fooled. Suppose I got flunked on this assignment for not showing up?

"Are you sure?" He was. So, there would be no classes tomorrow and probably the next as well because the streets would have to be cleared for cars and buses. Emergency vehicle routes always got first dibs.

"Listen for the No School Report," he said and abruptly hung up.

All right.

Thinking about those weekly Review sessions, they couldn't be legitimately classified as help, but it was all we had. The instructor would frown, rip away at the content of the painting, ignore or criticize our technique, but omit any useful suggestions as to what the student could do to make the painting better. That was life in my art school. Was it different elsewhere? Build a rocket, go someplace new, make friends with the natives, and try it there? Well, it was a thought.

When I was little there were no more wondrous words from the radio than the No School Report. That meant hot chocolate, baking cookies with Mommy, and watching B-westerns. Outside were howling winds and mounting inches of snow until the living room window was half covered. Waiting for Dad to make it home from work that first night was always a cliff-hanger. Then he would arrive, shake off the snow, sit down on the couch, and give us the dreadful details of the dangerous drive. It was great. If the storm was really serious, we'd sit around the living room together (often in the dark, if the power lines went down) and we'd be more or less huddled by the radio. We ate on TV trays. If the TV managed to keep broadcasting, we watched until we were bleary-eyed. If not, then it was just radio report after radio report—all the towns around Boston getting the shit kicked out of them by the horrible weather.

Then, usually a few days later, when the back of the storm was broken, my mother would suit me up for playing outside. This was a requirement. "You *will* go outside and get some fresh air," her way of saying *she* needed *some peace and quiet after being trapped indoors trying to keep me entertained.*

There was snowman building, snowball throwing, and snow angel making. And I always enjoyed watching the expeditions of ill-dressed neighbors plunging along the mostly unshoveled sidewalks, going to the store, the unfortunate result of not having stocked up. Not us. Our pantry was full.

Back inside again and all warmed up, I would eye the sagging power lines overhead as they looped down the street, heavily draped with snow and ice. Watching the Water and Power guys was pretty good stuff. Fooling with all that electricity. All that and no school. It was heaven.

The clattering window brought me back to the present. Huddled in my chair, I wondered why I was always required to prove myself, to explain why I selected certain symbols, why I chose a particular color. Over and over. Again and again. More proof. And more.

Maybe it wasn't any of their business. How about that?

Anyway, since the gods were giving me a reprieve, I decided I wouldn't quarrel with its form. I could stand a few days of no school. I would use the free time to focus on the next painting. Then maybe I wouldn't end up getting clobbered in Review next time.

I made myself a toasted tuna sandwich and a big cup of tea and sat in my chair until the wee hours of the morning. Listening to the radio was a lot like listening to a baseball game broadcast. I went to bed thinking everything was going to be fine.

DAY THREE

I was wrong.

The storm had come that night. Like Vulcan striking his anvil with a hammer of god-like proportions. There was no "next day." The city was smothered in violent darkness. The storm stayed and stayed and howled and raged.

It slammed viciously at everything in sight. It threw all its force against us pitiful humans in our pitiful hovels. It shook us until our teeth rattled. It buried the city with a speed that was breathtaking. It dealt its hand with frightening madness. It had no sense of time. No schedule to keep. It captured nearly every thought, every neuron. There were times when I thought the end of the world was upon me. We were outgunned so quickly. Power lines held for a few hours, then gave up and sank ignominiously to the ground, beaten and useless. We were buried in darkness: no heat, no phones, and many feet of snow.

Just once I cracked open my apartment door and peeked out to see. An enormous drift of snow was holding the front door of the building open. The wind had nearly ripped it off its hinges. Snowdrifts had rampaged in and filled the front hallway.

I shut my door again before the wind found me out.

The fury of the storm drove down the temperature in my apartment to an insane 45 degrees. The buildup of wet snow outside was freakish. It went up by the foot and kept climbing. It covered both windows. I was hemmed in on all sides.

Was there a chance I could actually suffocate? I sat trapped in my chair, the darkness abated by a few flickering candles.

Our city was cut off from the rest of the world.

One lone radio tower managed to keep its signal going with a backup generator because the two men who happened to be working up there that day had decided to wait a little longer before leaving for the night. When they understood that no one else was broadcasting, they stayed on the air relaying information that came through by hookup. They rested by turns. And ran out of food. In the end, they were exhausted and croaking with hoarseness. And they were heroes.

On the afternoon of the third day we listeners were stunned to hear the unexpected sound of a door being knocked on and the newscasters hollering out, "My God! Someone's at the door! Is it food?" They had been temporarily rescued from starvation by an ordinary citizen who decided to bundle up—like Admiral Byrd at the North Pole—and *crawl on all fours* to the skyscraper where the radio station had their office. Then he climbed about 100 flights of stairs with sandwiches and thermoses of coffee loaded in his backpack, declined an interview or to give his name, and then hiked down the 100 flights to somehow crawl home again.

Who knew that listening to hungry people gobbling sandwiches and slurping liquids would be worthy subjects fit for broadcast?

It felt good to cheer about something while the weather was going crazy. It was terrible to find out that some people only lived because their dogs kept them warm.

I dressed around the clock in triple layers of clothing. I was also lucky because, although it broke the law, I was able to use my gas stove to get a little heat going. Even though the windows were bolted, I certainly didn't have to worry about fresh air. My door rattled, the windows shook, and I already knew the front entrance to the building had been violated. Food was sardines and crackers, soup and hot tea. I just hoped I would live through the hours and days ahead.

The wind howled insanely. Our formerly solid brick building trembled under the onslaught. It was the coldest cold I had ever felt. The many hours of snowfall pressed down on me. I mostly sat or slept in my chair and kept my mittened hands warm by holding mugs of hot tea. A lot of the time was spent listening to the radio.

DAY FOUR AND BEYOND

The storm finally ended.

I knew we citizens had been suitably humbled. Who would have predicted our tolerating with such mild humor the marshal law imposed on us for the month that followed?

It was bitter cold my first day outside. The sky was a solid gorgeous blue and the sun blindingly bright. Standing in the negative space caused by the rakish tilt of a permanently wrecked steel-frame glass door, I found myself face to face with snow drifts eight to ten feet high. A wall of snow. End of story. I breathed in some air, which nearly froze my lungs, and hustled back inside to recover.

The next time I ventured out, I was dressed for the arctic, determined to get to the supermarket—if it was open. Normally it was a 20 minute walk. I was bundled up. I felt ready. To my surprise the front steps had been shoveled to the sidewalk. With some interest I saw there was now a narrow passage where the street used to be. It was a one-person-wide tunnel which led towards a three-street intersection in the distance. I had no idea what I would find when I got there but I was going to try.

It was like exiting from a spaceship crash and wondering if there were any other survivors. As I trudged along, I wondered who the intrepid tunnel-makers had been who had so graciously made it possible to go anywhere at all. Because, other than the tunnels, the only option would have been to scale the walls of the tunnel and walk around "up top." Supposing that the surface was safe enough. I did climb up once before I set out for that distant intersection, saw what looked exactly like every picture I've ever seen of the arctic—miles of snow in every direction—and climbed back down again. I didn't dare risk getting stuck somewhere or end up in a cave-in.

I also didn't feel comfortable walking on top because I knew there were cars buried underneath. Very creepy. So, it was use the tunnel or use nothing and stay home. I wasn't staying home. I couldn't stay inside another day or I would turn into a screaming freak.

Breathing the frigid air gingerly, I was both exhilarated and concerned by the time I reached the intersection that I might get worn out before I got to the supermarket. There would be no one to rescue me. While I tried to decide what to do, I looked around. Snowplows had carved out several one-car-wide lanes, thereby cutting lines in the blanket of snow. Who knew how far down the street the open car lane continued. I saw a plow smoothing down one of the makeshift arteries so, with a wave of my arm, I hailed him and he stopped. I was the only person on the street. It was impossible to miss me. Carefully picking my way across the deep gouges made by the few vehicles allowed to travel through, I had a momentary insight into how our pioneer forefathers must have felt taking their wagons out west, seeing the huge wheels make their first cuts in rough virgin land.

The plowman told me there was one lane open as far as the market. "A lotta people need food," he said. "You won't be alone." I waved goodbye and watched him turn the big yellow machine in the other direction. Kind of like "Martian Chronicles" stuff.

Entering that one-person-wide tunnel heading in the direction of the store, I slogged along. It was beautiful outside. It was bright. The sun was astounding. The sky was spectacular. And I was alive.

After two hours of hiking I reached my destination. Hot with the effort, I unzipped my jacket. Nanook of the North. With my hat off, the wind felt free to nibble my ears.

Outside the store was an apron of flattened-down snow. This made for easier walking and I joined a conga line of people which proceeded without faltering all the way through the store and out again, with hardly a hitch. Even married people weren't allowed to stand side by side. That was strange. But then again, seeing National Guardsmen with drawn weapons was strange. Each person was allowed to buy one box of dry milk and one loaf of bread. No stopping, no questions, just pay and keep going. At least I now knew first-hand what it must be like to live in Soviet Russia, although there would be no profiteering and no one tried to jump the line. No one in a fur coat tried to saunter in front just because they had fancier gear. In and out in about an hour, then I hiked home. This certainly was a different life than the one before the storm.

AFTERMATH

Life stayed different for some time. And it was getting interesting. I wasn't entirely against the new arrangement—for a while. We learned that out by the seaboard many homes had been wrecked, windows shattered. Going to the beach would mean being on "broken glass patrol" for a long time to come. Also the sea walls had been breached. Some damage had been expected, but in this case most of the fine, beautiful sand which our local beaches were famous for had been dragged up and pushed across the roads, covering the vegetation, and smeared against the sides of homes along with the snow. That was the status both up and down our part of the coast. As I said, things were a mess but mostly we were all alive.

The wildest human scene had been the thousands of motorists trapped during their evening commute the first night of the blizzard when traffic had simply ground to a halt in less than an hour. A few initial medical emergencies were helicoptered out but mostly people opted to live in their cars right there on the freeway for the next three days, except for a few who abandoned their cars and hiked home. Naturally one lady had her baby while fellow motorists handled the finer points of the delivery. There was no way the highway could be plowed.

During the storm, I had no time to think about Reviews. Afterwards, like everyone else, there was a period of adjustment to take into account all the changes. Classes didn't start again for another whole week. Actually, that little "vacation" sent the school administration into a tizzy because they had to figure out how to squeeze in those missing classes. We were to find ourselves spending two weeks in June making up the time, much to our collective student dismay.

Anyway, for sure it was evident that priorities had been reordered. For instance, I noticed that people were being extremely polite to each other. I don't remember another time when life was so winnowed down to basics and people so gracious. People were important again. Chatting while waiting for traffic to pass and lights to change became normal. We were fellow citizens, not combatants.

It was fun in other ways, too. I was aware that all outdoor movement was marked by the trekking of millions of pairs of feet through the icy, narrow passages dug by the intrepid. Those tunnels were the only way to get around. Otherwise it was snow as far as the eye could see—from the ground up, from one side of the street to the other. Looking at the apartment buildings across the street, they were buried right up to the second story. If one wanted to get to the other side of the street, that meant climbing up onto the now-hardened snow, supported by the frozen hulks of abandoned cars lining both sides of the street. Then one could cross (very gingerly) the frozen tundra in between and scale back down into the tunnel on the other side of the street. I quickly figured out there was nothing so pressing that I needed to go through all that. Also just walking down the street had taken on a whole new meaning, too, because inevitably it meant suffering the embarrassment of being squashed into a wall of snow by the body of a passing stranger or climbing on top of the embankment if it was agreed that the other "went first." There were no alternatives. It was that or stay inside your apartment. Not many wanted to stay inside. So people got used to it until the sidewalks were finally shoveled open again, which took a long time.

Oh yeah. Our city definitely looked like the proverbial arctic wastes.

THE MELTDOWN

Queer to think how the storm had made democrats of us all. Privilege meant nothing. We foot soldiers of the economy were the least impacted. We were used to walking. For those used to driving, it must have been agony since personal cars were forbidden. Only emergency service vehicles had permission to use the few cleared streets. Those who owned parked cars were forced to wait until late spring, months later, when the last of the impacted ice melted. Then new and used car sales and tow truck business boomed.

People who had the equipment for it traveled by snowshoes or skis. People didn't have a lot to do after the storm except shovel their sidewalks and hang loose because nothing was open except the hospitals. Later on, it was entertaining to see banker-types dressed in overalls and parkas. And in the meantime, since we were on an enforced vacation, we made the most of it. Like the daredevils who crossed the frozen river on foot. There was always an interested gallery to cheer when they made it across or to command a team to haul them out if the ice broke.

Life became inventive like that. After a while we were able to cross the river the conventional way, by the bridges, where the sidewalks were open because people simply trampled the snow into some semblance of passability.

The first Sunday after the storm it took half a day of walking to reach a restaurant I liked on the other side of the river. I wasn't sure it would be open, but I went anyway. It was something to do. It was an adventure. When I got there, it turned out about six or seven people had the same idea. An hour of banging on the door was resolved by the owner sticking his head out and telling us to go home. We laughed. Of course we weren't leaving. We were hungry. We wanted our breakfast. It took a considerable amount of persuasion but we finally convinced him to let us in. We had to swear to God that we wouldn't tell anyone about our lucky meal because he "wasn't open."

I walked home with a load of yummy food in my stomach and a doggy bag in my backpack. The treats would help assuage the cold hike across the bridge as the wind blew mercilessly. I felt like a frozen lollipop by the time I got home.

I also noticed that people were becoming a lot more robust due to the many hours of daily walking required to get to jobs or school.

The last reminders of the storm came when owners were finally able to chip out the useless metal carcasses of their cars in April or May.

Sometimes nothing prepares one for a storm like that. The test presents itself and one is tested. It can change a person.

It changed me. After the storm my behavior at school altered. I found myself more and more unwilling to adjust my work simply based on the critiques of instructors who presumed to know. Or maybe it was the insouciance gained from having survived the storm. The fact is that when I had first started art school, I was more like a blank page in an open book. *Write on me*, my eyes would say. When an instructor said, "You should change that," I would change whatever it was he was being critical of.

But after the storm, when he said, "That's wrong. Paint it this way," and then dared to approach my easel, his brush loaded with my paint, I blocked his way. The barbarian. How dare he!

"Whatever," he mumbled and backed away.

I stopped being as interested in praise when my instructor couldn't say why he liked a work.

Although I didn't voice it to myself, I had developed the idea that I would stand by the work I did. I would somehow learn to survive the criticism and the complaints about my newly unbending nature. More and more I did work that suited me. And I started taking chances—like when I worked on large sheets of good paper, gesturing in wide strokes of pastel color during life class, while the rest of the wretches were bent in their seats, subjugated to their careful 2H pencil drawings on cheap newsprint.

The subject matter of my photographs changed, too. And I was writing, and reading material not part of the curriculum. I was not trying to fit in so much. And in this way I was blossoming and I felt it.

I had new hope that I would still be me when I graduated. School would not modify me beyond recognition, which was what had been happening before the storm.

What I understand now is that somehow, around the time of that storm—the storm of the century—I started standing up for myself as a painter.

And what about the painting on my easel or the Review which the storm had interrupted? A week after the storm ended, our classes resumed. For some reason my painting fared better than usual. I didn't feel like I needed the validation but it was nevertheless true that my heart was buoyed because the painting instructor said I showed promise. Of course at the *next* Review the instructor reverted to his same old crabbiness, but there's nothing like success to leverage one out of the trough of despair. I would rise above the effect of the critiques—those that favored me, and those that didn't. I had decided I would keep painting anyway. When my four years in school ended I knew I would keep going as an artist.

Right now, it's winter—again. Outside my window it is snowing—again. How bleak it gets when the dark presses in so early in the day. Then I must be the light. I can do it. I can live through another winter. It's the price we pay to have a glorious spring.

As artists we select our own symbols to hold our own truths in place and every effort is worth the final result. There's no way to calculate the impact on the history of our world, the alteration to our culture, if every artist had knuckled under. Many have. We can weep for the loss. But many have stayed the course, against all odds. We don't know all the names. We only know a few. But they are each and every one of them great people. They help lift us up so we can stand on their shoulders and see into the future. Their desire is to help us reach our goals.

I think my direction as an artist was clearly in me before, but it was mostly locked inside. After the storm passed, I began to let it out. Now, being a survivor of that outrageous blizzard, I am like a warrior artist—determined to stay the course.

The work I do will bear witness. Even if other storms of magnitude try to overwhelm me, the fact is, I'm still here.

AUTHOR'S NOTE:

That wild experience cured me of New England winters and I moved to Los Angeles the summer after I graduated from college, in 1980. When I wrote my story, it was done from memory alone and from a distance of twenty years after the event. But it wasn't until *after* I had written my story that I decided to go on the internet and see what kind of reports existed. Had I blown the experience out of proportion? I was very pleased to find out I had gotten all the main points right. There was plenty to confirm that it was, indeed, The Storm of the Century—and I had lived to tell the tale. I was a true survivor.

The following is a compilation and distillation of articles I found on the internet. This little bit of scholarship will perhaps give the reader some idea of what the startled citizens of Boston and Cambridge, Massachusetts, themselves were confronted with when Mother Nature got riled up, back in February 1978.

The Blizzard of 1978 formed on February 5, and broke up on February 8. In all, up to 55 inches of snow fell in some areas. At the time, there was no comparable storm in the memory of the people of New England. It formed after three air masses merged into one: one mass over western Pennsylvania, another over northern Georgia, and the third over the Atlantic off the coast of North Carolina. *They all then converged over New England.*

The storm's incredible strength was sustained by near-hurricane level winds of approximately 65 mph and the formation of an eye-like structure located in the middle of the storm. A typical Nor'easter brings steady snow for 6 to 12 hours; this storm brought snow for a full 33 hours without let-up.

Over 3,500 cars were found abandoned and buried in the middle of roads during the clean-up effort. This figure does not include the countless other vehicles buried in driveways, on the sides of streets, and in parking lots.

In Boston and Cambridge, Massachusetts, automobile traffic was banned. Thousands of people walked around the quiet city streets and frozen Charles River, some on cross-country skis.

There were snow drifts of up to 15 feet in some places. The blizzard notably brought out a feeling of camaraderie, as it affected everyone equally. The Blizzard of '78 also eventually gave birth to a tradition in southern New England known as the "bread and milk runs." This was because when frantic people went to the supermarket, all the bread and milk that the markets had were gone in a flash.

Amy L. reported on Homepage Journal in 2001, "The only way people could leave their house was to go out of their windows because their doors had become blocked from all of the snow that had built up." Harvey Leonard, Chief Meteorologist for WHDH-TV commented in a CNN interview on April 25, 2001, "Once the storm hit, the actual act of traveling by automobiles was declared illegal. It paralyzed Boston for a solid four days: quarantines on driving, marshal law kind of an institution."

when Joe Blows

CATHERINE MCGUIRE

Catherine McGuire has had more than 200 poems published in venues such as *Adagio, Folio, Fireweed, FutureCycle, Green Fuse, New Verse News, Nibble, Portland Lights Anthology, The Quizzical Chair Anthology, The Smoking Poet,* and *Tapjoe.* Her chapbook, *Palimpsests,* was published by Uttered Chaos in 2011. She is webmaster for the Oregon Poetry Society and has two self-published chapbooks. Her website is www.cathymcguire.com.

Wherever pressure is applied
there is uncertainty—a thick steel wall
will buckle, blast, blow.
Afterwards they blame weak welds.

The screws applied and tightened
the pressure builds each day:
what one of us sits easy? Layoffs, illness,
family feuds, foreclosures—see the steam rise.

Decades of dancing on razors, skating
on cracking ice; our muscles groan.
The scream rises, is choked back.
But who has checked each and every weld?

The "mad as hell" are letting loose—
a brain blast melts their off switch
and their madness shrapnels
the neighborhood with real lead.

Enough is Enough

LYLANNE MUSSELMAN

Lylanne Musselman is an award-winning poet and painter living in Toledo, Ohio. She teaches writing of all stripes at Terra State and Owens Community Colleges. Her work has appeared in *Pank Magazine*, *Tipton Poetry Journal*, and *New Verse News*, among other publications. She is the author of two chapbooks: *A Charm Bracelet for Cruising* (Winged City Press, 2009) and *Winged Graffiti* (Finishing Line Press, 2011).

Storms have always been a nemesis
across Mother Earth, but here in the Midwest
they pick on us—
imposing bullies who won't quit
until we cry "uncle,"
forcing us to dig deeper storm cellars,
build higher levees,
and restock disaster supply kits.
We plan our escapes,
flash storm watches and warnings,
see the hopeful rainbow—
so we stick it out, vulnerable,
surrounded by corn and bean fields,
helpless as the cows and horses,
but it's only a matter of time
before thunderheads boil across the horizon,
smother the sun and propel winds into killers—
uproot century-old trees, trample flowers,
flood crops, slay livestock, and ransack our homes.
We return from our hideouts to find
that signed copy of *Breakfast of Champions* destroyed,
that photo of Aunt Mildred ruined,
the neighbor's Chevy Silverado flipped into town hall,
that manuscript, nearly complete after twenty-five years, gone,
and, Tabby, missing for days,
crawls out from under the overturned armoire.

the approach of doom

HENRIK RAMSAGER

Henrik Ramsager has recently appeared in such anthologies as *Cutlass and Musket*, *Discovery*, *Midnight Showdown*, and *Spirit Legends*. He was the winner of the Rogue Blades Entertainment *Challenge! Discovery 2010* anthology contest.

THE SEA WAS RESTLESS BENEATH THE DARKENING SKY.
For many minutes Rurik Longmane, jarl of five hundred men and
seven ships, had looked eastward at the rising band of darkness.
The signs that he read in the distance were ominous. What he saw
there was reflected in the harsh lines and clenched teeth of his face.

Standing beside him under the dragon-headed prow of Rurik's
flagship was a bearish-looking man, Aun—rash, bold, and battle-
scarred.

"Can we outrun it?" asked Aun. "Already the headland to the
northwest is within sight. The leeside will shelter us 'til the storm
has passed."

Rurik spat over the side of his ship into the gusting wind.

"We won't be halfway across before the storm overtakes us," was
the grim answer.

"Let us do something," snarled Aun, easily frustrated when a
problem could not be solved with his battleaxe.

Whatever it was that Rurik answered in reply was lost to the sharp,
raw crackle of thunder that sounded above. The minutes passed.
A fresh, driving wind began to buffet the ship, quickly picking up
strength until it howled in their ears and sent shudders through the
mast and keel. Time and again, those who worked the sweeps felt
their oars wrenched from their hands. As the mast swayed and the
sail bellied, the shrouds began to break loose, but the mast held.
With the wind came the swelling of the waves. The water sprayed
and churned more fiercely with each passing moment. Waves that
were like geysers leapt up and came crashing down across the face
of the deck. Rurik set the men to bailing. Here Aun had his answer
for what could be done.

It came rapidly now: a flying, raging, tumultuous film was clos-
ing on them. In the darkness Rurik had already lost sight of all but
one of his other ships.

Some men laughed. Some fell to their knees between the cross-
beams and wept. Others clutched their hammer-shaped amulets
and prayed to Thor, god of thunder and storms, or to Ægir, god of
the cruel sea, who lived in his hall far beneath the waves. But however they reacted, each man saw the doom that approached.

"Down sail!" shouted Rurik, but it was from the reading of his hand gesture that his order was obeyed. Staggering down the length of his rocking ship like a drunkard, Rurik reached his steersman and helped him to steady the steering oar so that the tail of the ship was to the approaching tempest.

For several minutes the ship ran swiftly before the wind. But it would not last.

Then, all at once, the full force of the sea storm plowed into them. The ship surged forward. For a moment, the ship was held straight against the onrushing tempest. Then it abruptly sheared into the waves and was spun and tossed about directionless, like a small toy. The larboard flank plunged low into the water. Men bailed frantically. Then the sea swelled as never before, rolling under the ship like hills. Riding the white-foamed crest of one of the largest waves to come, the ship nearly overturned in its wake. Two of the crewmen were tossed clear of the deck straight into the waters, never to be seen again. Another was flung across the breast of the ship against the bulwark, then over the side. For a moment he clung to the railing by his feet alone, then was torn free. With his arms extended above his head, it looked as if he had purposely gone for a dive when he hit the water.

A great, thunderous clap heard above even the roar of the tempest heralded the breaking of the mast. As the mast was swept overboard, most of the rigging and two more souls entangled in the shrouds went with it.

Suddenly, through the dark, murky chaos, Rurik sighted the mainland. They were closer to the coast than he'd thought possible. Or perhaps the storm had simply picked them up and catapulted them to this new point.

Death lurked just ahead. A swirling flood of water and foam brought the ship into a narrow strait between two islands. Treacherous rocks were on either hand. The bow scraped against something unseen. The crew were hurled forward, then back again. A bilge strake from the outer hull was shorn off. But still they sped onward into the gulf. Dark, brackish water and mud rushed past the ship. Tangled flotsam—no doubt from Rurik's six other ships—kept pace with the ship at each side.

The worst seemed over, yet it was not. Ahead was a mass of rocks, jutting from the wild foaming waters like the fangs of a waiting sea serpent.

Rurik thumped the shoulder of Aun, who was somehow at his side again. Rurik pointed to the horror that lay ahead. Both began tearing off their helmets and armor. Others of the crew followed suit. The waters of the sea awaited, and it was a common saying that where the sea was concerned, an armored man is a dead man.

Driven into the crags, the once-proud vessel cracked and splintered. Amid the noise and wild spray of water, the crew were hurled from the dying ship and scattered in every direction.

Men who had come to conquer a foreign land were themselves conquered by the sea before they had even reached its shore. These were the thoughts of some as the sea swallowed them.

⸏

Rurik was awakened by a kick to his side. "Arise, you Danish dog!"

Still weak from his ordeal, he looked up into the face of his enemy, a Northumbrian man with a dark, crumbling set of teeth. He noticed that the man wore Rurik's two gold armbands but that they hung loose on his wrists, for the Northumbrian had too little muscle for them to fit snugly further up the arms. After an outbreak of coughing, Rurik brought up a tankardful of brine.

As he struggled up into a seated position, Rurik discovered that his hands were bound behind his back by coarse-woven hemp. Looking past his tormentor, he saw that he was not the only survivor from the storm. Perhaps thirty or thirty-five members of his crew were likewise tied up. They knelt close together in a line, tired and defeated, a few paces away. Surrounding them were several dozen angry-looking men. Most of them, judged Rurik, had the look of farmers. There were also a dozen or so hard-nosed soldiers. The soldiers had spears and a few had swords. The farmers bore axes, hoes, or cudgels. Four or five had swords, no doubt captured from his crew. Rurik wondered if any of his men from the other six ships had survived.

His eyes then fell upon Aun staring back at him. He was on the ground at the knees of his shipmates. At first Rurik thought he was resting on his side. Then he realized that Aun was dead. A gaping wound was in his stomach. *How like him it would be*, thought Rurik, *to resist being taken alive, even if he was half-dead from the sea storm.*

"Up, I said!" growled the Northumbrian with the bad teeth a second time.

With eyes that blazed and a snarl in his throat, Rurik looked up at the man, who took a step back, clearly intimidated. Then, remembering that his prisoner was bound, he drew back the shaft of his spear and was about to thump Rurik in the chest with the blunt end, when a voice restrained him. "Stay, brother. There is no need for violence."

It was the voice of a holy man, one of the shepherds of the White Christ's followers. Clad in their brown cowls and with their heads tonsured, several of them had ventured to the kingdom of the Danes. There they had tried to convey news of their god. But few people bothered to listen to what sounded like the ravings of men who had been too long out in the sun. The White Christ priests were killed or else enslaved, their silver crucifixes torn from their necks. Those who were enslaved proved to be poor servants. Word of their ineffectiveness spread, and when the next wave came, they were summarily killed or else driven away. Those who could sing well, however, were highly prized by their new masters.

The holy man standing over Rurik smiled. "Come, Daneman, stand up," he urged, speaking gently to him in his own language. "Join your brethren yonder. A wonderful event is about to take place."

Rurik rose sluggishly to his feet. His head swam and his stomach was in a wretched state. "Who are you?" asked Rurik, his tone defiant.

"I am he whose pleasure it is to be your host—of a kind—and, if it is God's will, your savior."

"I need no saving, priest, if that is what you are."

"I am called Joshua, a humble man of God," he continued, as if he had not heard what Rurik said. "Near this shore lies a monastery—pillaged, it is true, by your kind in years past, but still standing. For stone walls strongly built endure where wood succumbs all too soon to flame. There at our monastery I serve as abbot."

"I do not know this word," said Rurik indifferently. "It sounds to me like you are a priest."

"I am, yea, but, more than this, I am the leader of the men who abide within its hallowed walls," replied the abbot, his pride unknowingly stung by Rurik.

"What do you want of us? You will kill us now, I presume?" said Rurik wearily.

"That depends on you, brother, and whether you would dwell in darkness or in light."

"What do you mean?" asked Rurik guardedly. As he spoke, he took a step closer and considered the damage he could inflict against the abbot with his feet before any of the abbot's people could come to his aid.

"Let me be your guide, Rurik Longmane. Aye, I have already been told your name," said the abbot, taking Rurik by the elbow. Observing that the jarl was unsteady on his feet, the abbot signaled for a monk to assist him at the other side.

When they had brought him to where the other Vikings were, the abbot said, "Kneel, Jarl Rurik Longmane of Jutland, son of Harald Thorarinsson. I am here to help you."

Rurik knelt alongside the others. "Help me?" he said, squinting as he looked up at the abbot.

"Aye, for you are in need of help, as are you all," he added, looking at the others. His voice rang with compassion as he folded his hands together.

The monk who had escorted Rurik likewise put his hands together, as did six other monks who were there. A prayer, spoken in Latin, was recited, which no one apart from the abbot and one or two of the monks understood.

"Brother Justin," said the abbot when they had finished, "bring forth the water."

"Father," complained the leader of the soldiers to the abbot, "let us soon be done with this. It is not wise to linger here."

"Patience, patience, Reeve," responded the abbot with infinite patience of his own as well as calmness. "We'll not be long. It is the Lord's work we do here—His bidding; and what is more important than that? Ah, here is Brother Justin."

The monk, carrying a wooden milking bucket full of water, set it down in front of Rurik. "Forgive me, Father. I could not find a barrel."

"It will have to do," answered the abbot. Then, looking at Rurik, he said, "It is time."

"Time for what?" asked the jarl.

"You have no equivalent word for it in your language, but in ours it is called a *baptism*. It is a simple and painless procedure in which your heads are splashed with water. At the end of it, you will be as us. You will be our brother Christians." The abbot looked beyond Rurik now as if he spoke to some wider, unseen audience. "It is said that the greater the sinner who embraces the Lord, the greater is the rejoicing of the angels in Heaven."

"Do I understand you correctly?" began Rurik. "You wish to wash us with that water and then expect us to become your friends?" Despite all the ill luck they'd suffered this day and were likely still to suffer, most of the Danes found it within themselves to laugh heartily at the abbot's proposal.

"It is not meet that you laugh where our Lord God is concerned," said the abbot in a suddenly ominous tone. "Do you not see that this is a part of your destiny? Do you not see that all that has befallen you this day has led you to this? Your gods have failed you today, whilst our God—the true God—has taken pity on us. The storm that arose today so suddenly is proof of what I say. God, in answer to our earnest prayers, sent it to smite you. Once you have agreed to be baptized, all that is required of you is to repent of your sins and vow to embrace your new Lord who stands waiting at Heaven's high altar."

"We do this, and you'll set us free?" asked Rurik.

The reeve and most of the monks and others looked at the abbot as if eager to see whether his expression would match his words. In the event, there were no words. The abbot merely locked his hands together again and nodded sagely.

The abbot collected a handful of water from the bucket and held it over Rurik. "Do you then, Rurik Longmane, repent of your earthly sins and accept Jesus Christ as your Lord?"

The jarl nodded his assent. What was it to him to acknowledge their strange god if it meant life.

The abbot sprinkled the baptismal water on the head of Rurik. "Praise God!" he declared. "Praise God!" echoed the monks.

With the help of the monks, the ceremony was hastily repeated for each of the others. It occurred to Rurik that they seemed to be in a hurry.

When it was done, the abbot stepped back and made the sign of the cross. The monks followed suit.

Looking at the reeve, the abbot then said, "Our work is done. You may proceed."

The bucket was removed and a chopping block from a nearby cottage was brought forward to replace it. One of the soldiers, a powerfully built man with a scar running along his brow stepped forward. Over his shoulder rested an axe. Two men seized the last Dane in the line from behind and forced his head down on the chopping block.

"Liar!" roared Rurik at the other end of the line at the abbot.

"My son," replied the abbot, who seemed to be at peace with what he had done, "you asked if you would be freed. Whilst your earthly bodies, it is true, are condemned to the block, I have contrived to save your immortal souls. In that sense, you are now free."

Rurik would have risen and rushed the abbot, but heavy hands restrained him from behind. The rest of the captives would also have risen, but the sharp press of spear or sword points at their backs kept them rooted to the ground.

"You Danes are wild—too wild to have here among us. Such as you cannot be suffered to live; but our gift to you is greater than life itself, for you will soon know the peace of God in His blessed kingdom." Turning now to the executioner, who had awaited the final signal of the abbot, the holy man gestured for the executioner to proceed. The reeve was displeased by this, as he saw it as an infringement of his authority, but said nothing.

The executioner raised his axe up high. The sharpened head caught the light that shined down from a rift in the clouds. The doomed Dane struggled against the two who held him, which momentarily spoiled the aim of the executioner. "Hold the bastard still," complained the executioner. With the captive again steady, the executioner's eye marked the exact line that would disconnect the head in one stroke or, he hoped, no more than two.

"Look!" interrupted a voice suddenly. The axeman turned and lifted his head. So too did the abbot, the monks, the reeve, the soldiers, and the farmers.

Rounding the headland were two ships. A moment later, a third, a fourth, and then one more appeared, each with a beast-headed prow. In all, here were five out of the original seven ships belonging to Rurik.

"The fleet! They survive after all!" cried one of the Danes.

Distracted by the sight, most of the Northumbrians who were restraining the prisoners relaxed their hold on their weapons. Fearing a spear in their backs at any moment, the Danes sprang to their feet and made a wild dash for the nearby ships. Three or four were cut down, but the rest were able to break free. The man on the chopping block, having twisted free of the two who had restrained him, began to roll away. The executioner brought down his axe but struck wide just as the Dane got to his feet and joined the others in the mad dash to get away. The two who had restrained him had already begun running inland, as had most of the other Northumbrians. Slow on his feet, one of the monks received an arrow in his back from the first of the new Danes who had landed and were coming up fast now. The executioner, one of the last to flee, was struck by an arrow in his calf but continued running.

Two or three hours later, most of the monks and a few of the others had been captured. Among their number was the abbot. The reeve, on horseback, had escaped. The rest had been killed or were in hiding. Like the Danes before them, the Northumbrian captives were made to kneel. Their positions were now reversed.

"Change me—change us all—back," ordered Rurik, poking the abbot's neck with the tip of his dagger.

The abbot shook his head emphatically. "Once done, it cannot be undone. You are now and forever of my faith. I have purged you of the evil that is inherent in you. I have watered the seed that was within you. Now you must allow it to sprout and grow."

"You should have killed me when you first had the chance," reflected Rurik.

"Mayhap it was Providence that I did not. Mayhap it is God's plan that you live and spread His word."

"Change me back," growled Rurik wolfishly, beginning to dig the point of his dagger into the abbot's neck.

With his life apparently hanging by a thread, the abbot finally relented. He called for the same bucket he'd used before. When it was placed on the ground, the abbot started to move toward it, but a rough hand pushed him back. He was then witness to the sight of the Danes placing the largest hammer amulet they had at the bottom of the bucket.

When the abbot, in a nervous, faltering tone, began to speak in Latin, the jarl barked to him that he was to use only the Norse tongue. Thereafter the abbot made sure to use the word "unbaptize" as many times as possible, since it seemed to have a calming effect on Rurik and his men.

The ceremony was repeated for each of the other Danes who had previously been baptized. As before, water was sprinkled on each of their heads.

"In the name of the Son, the Holy Spirit, and"—he hesitated—"Odin, I now pronounce each of you unbaptized," declared the abbot with authoritative finality. The interjection of "Odin" pleased the Danes, and, to their minds, lent an added air of authenticity to the ceremony.

"Now, there is one more ceremony to perform," announced Rurik. The abbot was dragged before him. From under his tunic, the jarl lifted up over his head his hammer amulet and rawhide string connected to it. "Our ceremony requires you to kiss the hammer of Thor."

"Nay, nay!" cried the abbot, turning his head away. His face contorted with disgust. "Ignorant savages! I am a man of God!"

"Now you shall be a man of Odin and the other gods that you formerly despised," said Rurik. "Kiss it!"

"Kiss it!" roared a couple hundred other voices.

The amulet was forced forward against the lips of the abbot while his head was held steady.

When the amulet was pulled away, the abbot let out a fearful shriek. The monks meanwhile began wailing and wringing their hands.

"*I embrace my new lord Odin and renounce my former lord.* Say it!" commanded Rurik.

As an inducement, the keen edge of Rurik's dagger was again brought to the abbot's throat and one of his arms was bent upward at the elbow behind his back.

"I embrace my new lord Odin and renounce my former lord!" cried the horrified abbot, drowning in anguish and torment. Having said these words, from which his very soul recoiled, the abbot sank to the ground with his hands covering his face in shame.

"In the name of the son of Odin, Odin himself, and also his good holy sensuous wife Freya, I pronounce you now and forevermore a brother of our religion and never again of your former religion." Rurik's words and the abbot's sobbing drew a great deal of laughter from the Danes.

Each of the monks was in turn forcibly converted from their religion in the same manner.

When the last monk had been converted, Rurik looked upon the huddled mass of misery at his feet. The abbot in particular seemed to be a broken man. He had meant to kill them after his impromptu initiation, but, seeing the state of torment it had induced, decided against it.

"Remember," said Rurik, "you are now bound forever to our gods. Your souls are burned with the mark of Odin and can never revert to the White Christ," he said sternly as he suppressed a laugh.

This communication seemed to send a fresh convulsion through those of the newly baptized who understood his language.

Two days later Rurik's remaining ships, laden with spoils, sailed down a nearby river that led out into the sea. Near the mouth of the river was the local monastery referred to earlier by the abbot. As they passed the walls of the monastery, they could hear the continual wailing and flagellating of the inmates. And outside the walls near the riverbank was the body of a monk hanging by the neck from a tree branch.

Plying their oars, the cheerful and contented crew of Rurik's longship broke into a rough-voiced song. The air was still, and the open sea lay just ahead.

the monster that eats up the sky

ANN CARTER

Ann has spent most of her working life as a Management Consultant in the United Kingdom. As a child, with Air Force parents, she lived in a number of exotic locations that included Aden and Singapore. As an adult, however, she has lived a more prosaic existence in Cornwall, Yorkshire, and Lincolnshire. Here she adores the traditional English countryside but sees how population growth and creeping urbanization are slowly eating away at England's two-thousand-year-old heritage. As an avid gardener and watercolor painter she extends that thread of creativity by writing poetry, using the medium to express her misgivings at the way we treat our environment and our unwillingness to knuckle down and put the world back to rights.

We saw it coming,
the monster that eats up the sky.
We saw it coming,
foolish greed was the reason why.
It kills our children,
it kills our women,
while we sit and stare as they die.

We know the reason,
why children are drowned in their sleep.
We know the reason,
that livestock falls sick to disease.
We could have stopped it,
we could have capped it,
but we carried on as we pleased.

We know it's coming,
the monster that eats up the sky.
We know it's coming,
but are we too stupid to try?
It'll kill our children.
It'll kill our women.
This creature we've made and let fly.

Is there a future,
for us and the rest of our kin?
Is there a future,
if we shrug and still do nothing?
We must do better,
and pull together,
to have any hope of winning.

Stop burning fuel,
is a ban we know we must make.
Oh yes it's cruel,
a bitter pill we know we must take.
Hope is not gone yet.
Will our young regret,
if we never correct this mistake?

FIRST PHANTASMA

JOSHUA DANIEL COCHRAN

Long before receiving an MFA from City College of New York, Mr. Cochran had been busy writing fiction, non-fiction, and poetry. His work has been published in a wide array of literary journals, trade magazines, travel guides, anthologies, and electronic media, and his first novel, *Echo Detained*, was published by Fractious Press (New York) in 2007. Most recently, Mr. Cochran's work has appeared in *The Blue Guitar* (2011), *Bourbon Penn* (2011), and *Skive Magazine* (Australia, 2010).

PROKOPYEVSK, SIBERIA
RUSSIA

With a pounding heart, she sits up in bed and a strange sound comes out of her throat—a little croaking moan of surprise and disappointment. She looks at the rumpled forms of her legs beneath the sheet, the little dapples of blue moonlight across the surface of her bed. *It seems even this was in the dream,* she thinks quickly, placing a hand across her heart and trying to calm her breath. Everything was in the dream: every possible feeling, every vision. She moves her legs slightly even against the pain, causing the pattern of light and deeper shadows to move and rustle. Looking around, she knows it's her room. Radka snores from all her medications in the neighboring bed. There are the same familiar things—the bedpan, the curtains around each bed, the red call button and blue hint of window somewhere beyond—and she feels a sense of calm come over her, a sense of sameness. Calm yes, but something impending too—a prickliness just out of reach. What if it had been true? What if it ever became true?

And still the dream. *The dream,* her mind pulls her back to it and she tries to remember. Visions and images recede as fast as she recalls them, falling apart through the darkness of memory like rotted gauze, smoky between her reaching hands. Faces. An impossible number of faces, everyone that ever was or would be. A kind of animalistic terror mixed with almost a delight, hope, endless water, endless space both outside and within. An unspeakable darkness, darkness stirred out into the light. The smell of the hidden revealed: wetness, of dried and dead sticks wetted in the rain, a strange blend of vigor and death and something...well, something good maybe. She feels as if something were about to happen, but she doesn't know where or how or why. Still, there are the sheets and their mazy shadows and she looks at them again for a while and slowly lies back down. Perhaps now she will die, allow the ever-growing weariness to finally wash over her. No more struggle. She wants to go back to sleep again, hopes she can quiet her heart and go back to sleep. She wants to get back to that place of dreaming, that place where it is all changed.

MENZIES, WESTERN OUTBACK
AUSTRALIA

The little girl wonders why it seems so strange today, why even *she* feels calmer, quieter. Class hasn't started, the teacher isn't even here. The few students who are sit at their desks. Amanda and Rex are talking in low voices. Sara and Piper have papers in front of them and write or draw. Paul is wearing his pajamas but it isn't funny for some reason and he stares into the air.

She looks to the window and sees morning out on the playground. The quiet and pale eucalyptus trees and the yellow paddocks beyond, the waiting swings, the fountain where she watches with the rest of the girls at recess. Looking at the fountain, she feels that calm and quiet like a warmth. *It's like seeing something you want*, she thinks. *It's like looking out this window and wanting to be out there, a calm like looking through a window and seeing a tree sway in the breeze but smelling nothing on the wind, feeling nothing against the cheek, not hearing the sound of the leaves stirring.*

And even the bus ride was quiet, she thinks. *There were only six of us. We each got our own seat, for once.* She looks at the scribbles carved into her desk. *The bus driver, Mr. Howard, didn't even have to yell at anybody on the long ride, not even Gabe, but only sat in his seat with his head crooked to the side like maybe he slept on it wrong but he moved it fine to open the door for everybody or turn around. When we passed the burning car he didn't even slow down. He maybe even smiled.*

⌇

It all seems so strange, like the dream kept going even after she opened her eyes. It took her a while to realize that she had even woken up for real. She got out of bed and wandered about her room for a while, looking at her belongings with the eyes of a stranger. She felt both happy and sad. Everything seemed to glow with a newness of color. The sun was bright and yellow, winking through the trees and falling in warm patches upon her body. She held out her hand in a chink of sunlight and moved so that it traced her arm. It tingled where it touched. Then she let it trace her other arm, across her nightgown, up her neck, and then it finally fell upon her face. The warmth was like beautiful music against her skin and she stood there, slightly hunched to catch the ray for a few minutes, smiling with closed eyes at the sun against her face. Then she wanted to go outside.

She crept out of her room, listening to the silence of the house. It was early. *Mum won't wake up until seven at least*, she thought, and then stopped. She realized she hadn't seen the sunrise since winter had gone, always sleeping in, sleeping late and being late and making Mum rush and fuss her out the door to the bus stop. But still, she wanted to go outside, so she made her way quietly down the stairs. The great sense of change in the house almost frightened her, as if everything were hollowed out. When she got downstairs, she decided to go out back, through the kitchen.

The figure standing at the door made her cry out. Her mom, turning at the sound, released her own scream and raised her hands to her face. The two of them stood there for a moment with widened eyes, both of them clasping themselves and staring. Her mom smiled, and then they both laughed. Her mother took her up in her arms and held her and they both giggled together for a while, not saying anything, just touching and smiling.

"You scared me, Melissa." Her mother pushed her back to regard her and brushed away a lock of errant hair.

But Melissa, looking up at her mother with that feeling of newness, the light through the window and waiting outside, could think of nothing to say. Instead, she opened the door and the two of them sat down on the step and watched the sunrise shattered through the hedgerow. The hedgerow that was supposed to block the outback winds but never seemed to do so. She didn't speak and her mom was silent too. Her mom made coffee and brought her some juice. They sat and watched and waited. When it fell against her body in little patches, the sun again felt like some golden promise. She was going to ask her mom about it but when she turned, her mom's eyes were shut and she was holding her hand out before her, completely relaxed and natural as if she did it all the time. In her palm, held cupped like for dipping water, there was a little shard of sunlight that had broken through the canopy of trees.

↝

When the teacher walks in, Melissa shakes the morning's memories from her mind the way she shakes water from her hair. *Mrs. Zimmer is late*, she thinks, looking up at the clock. *And still, the few of us here just sit quietly, even more quiet now and waiting.*

"I'm sorry to have kept you waiting. I—" She looks out into the room, slowly making eye contact with each of the faces before her, faintly smiling. "I think we should do something different today," she says and nods to herself. "Yes. Something entirely different."

TETUAN, TETUAN PROVINCE
MOROCCO

Little puffs of dust wisp from his pattering feet and swirl and fade into the air behind him. He doesn't even have to try to run. His heart won't stop beating, not since this morning. His eyes widen with the memory of his brother waking him with the terrible screams—mouth foaming, Father having to tie him and lock him in the closet as he screamed and raved, as blood flowed across his face. And before that, the dream. So wondrous and vast.

The boy's legs burn from the strain of running, having first scrabbled nearly a mile through the maquis toward his uncle Saul's house on the hill with the cypress stand around the well, then down and through the thicket of pine at the property edge where the Berber family kept their smoky camp, strangely deserted though, and now along the lumpy road from his uncle's house toward the home of his grandfather another two miles to go. Dawn hasn't yet broken and he hopes to make it before Azan. Black fingers of smoke rise in the distance, towards the city. Though his grandfather lives closer to town, the mosque is still very far away and difficult to hear along the wind because the muezzin is so very old. It would be improper for him to show up during Salah. He would be punished severely, he knows, for missing the call to prayer. He kicks his legs on further though they burn with effort. The image comes again. His brother scratching out his own eyes before Father could stop him and lock him away.

When he made it to his uncle's house earlier, the moon had still been up and hovering like a sickle over the rounded hills that led up into the blue peaks to the east. Crickets rasped and night was slowly succumbing to the world of day. Birds chittered and fluttered in anticipation amongst the wild heather and rosemary that led up the final slope toward Saul's house. His uncle's dog, a mean and terrifying mongrel that always tried to bite him, didn't even bark as he approached the house and as he got closer he could make out the forms of people standing outside as if admiring the moon, the dog lying idle at their feet. When he came upon them, they turned to him and muttered *salam* almost in unison, even his two cousins. The dog panted and stared at him.

He had stopped before them gasping, heart bounding, trying to speak but the dryness in his throat made him cough. His uncle told him to calm down and made his younger daughter go and fetch water. The boy stood there trying to regain his breath for a few moments before he could even swallow. His uncle came over to him and put out his arm and enveloped the boy in his flowing robe.

"It's going to be all right, Ahmed," his uncle said, smiling down at him. "You were sent here by your father." It was not a question.

The boy could only nod. He wanted to tell his uncle about Hassim, how he screamed, but he could only take the bowl of water held before him with widened eyes and drink deeply, still breathing hard through his nose, until the bowl was empty. His uncle patted him on the back and knelt down and told him that he had to continue on to Grandfather's house, to make sure it had come there too.

So he runs along the dusty road. It turns to a rough asphalt now and grows more and more dense with whitewashed buildings squatting on either side; so very close. The sky is filled with smoke in the distance. He notices other people up and about. A group of women in full hijab hustle by talking loudly. An older boy, nearly a man, runs by Ahmed going in the opposite direction, equally as breathless and staring at the ground rushing up before him as if hypnotized, covered in another's blood. Ahmed's legs still burn, but that's not on his mind. When he turns the corner, his grandfather is standing there in the street as if he's been waiting for him to arrive all this time. And just then, the call of the muezzin comes strong and clear through the dawn air growing orange in the east. His grandfather smiles a toothless smile and waves Ahmed into his arms.

LONDON, ENGLAND

"That's the most ridiculous thing I've heard in a long time, I'm sorry," he says into the phone. And he really is sorry. His mother seems to get more and more mystical the older she gets. "Really, I'm sorry, but I have to go now. Why don't you go back to sleep?" He holds up a finger to a man standing in the doorway dressed in a blue suit like his own, but wrinkled and frumpled. The other sits down facing him in a disheveled heap. "Okay, Mum. Yes, I'll try to do that." He rolls his eyes. "Okay, Mum. Bye-bye, dear." He hangs up with a little shake of his head.

"Morning," the man sitting before him mumbles with a wave of the hand. "I know this is important, but I can't stay long, Seth. I've got to go back home. Is your mum all right?" the other asks, shifting his leather notebook from one hand to the other and taking out a pen. He clicks it ready and opens the notebook.

"God, yes," he says. "A little hysterical, but that's all."

"Hysterical," the other repeats.

"Yeah, she's had a lot of trouble since Dad passed. No big thing, I suppose." He gathers up the Palmer files and opens them, looking down the columns but seeing only numbers that look like nothing, like hieroglyphs—little unknown symbols. It's only four a.m. and he hasn't gotten any sleep, having worked straight through the night putting numbers together, taking them apart. In a panic, he even called the entire crew at midnight to schedule an emergency meeting.

But something his mother said about her dream kindled something in him. He's slightly bothered by it, annoyed, that's all. His mother and all these damn changes. She called him one day and told him that she was a lesbian, just like that. One day she converted to Buddhism. It was insanity. Lost in such thought, he looks up and the other man, Stevens, is staring at him. "What is it?" he says.

"Well, it's just that my mother called me too—in the middle of the night, from her holiday in Venice—and my wife was...um... acting strange this morning when I got up to get ready for work."

"Your wife?"

"Yeah, well, me too, I guess." Stevens shifts in the chair and clicks his pen out of waiting. His hair, usually slicked back with something, is dry and falls around his face. "You've been watching the news, right?"

"Telly's gone," Seth says.

"Oh, well…" Stevens seems to choke on a few words.

"What is it?"

"It's just that...that the world is changing. That's all. It's on all the stations, the ones that still work. I don't even know why I came this morning. My wife wanted me to stay home." He stares out at the sky graying now with the dawn. "It's coming here too. It's rolling across the—"

"What the bloody hell are you talking about?" Seth interrupts. "Is this why Rachel, Morgan, and what's-his-name aren't here?"

"The change is rolling across the entire world and…" Stevens acts as if he might say more but stops.

"What's happened?" But Stevens won't look at him. He only stares out the window with a puzzled, lost expression. Seth bites his lip and leans back with a creaking of his chair and looks out the window with him, to the space above the streets of London, the other buildings in the distance. Ghostly hues of gold and orange begin to tinge the grey sky. A column of smoke rises black and ominous on the horizon but Seth pays it no mind. He actually wants to ask Stevens something, but doesn't want to feel like an idiot.

"So, what about the Palmer audit?" Stevens says suddenly. "Let's get this over with." He blinks and again clicks his pen and looks at his notebook on his leg as if it might speak. They both are quiet for a while as they look at the papers before them, shuffling them dryly and rearranging them. Someone clears his throat.

"All right," Seth says suddenly, looking up. "So what did you dream about?"

"What?"

"I suppose you had loopy dreams?" he asks, impatient.

"Oh, I don't know. It's hard to explain really. Everyone was there, approving, judging—" He furrows his brow at some recollection. "But *participating* too. It was vivid though," Stevens says with a certain brightness. "And the sky! I've never dreamt like this before." He smiles and looks out the window. Another tendril of smoke has begun.

"Like what?" Seth asks quietly.

"I don't know," Stevens says as if lost in thought and wandering. When he speaks again, his voice is just breath. "There was so much space, a sky within me…"

Seth watches the blankness on his face for a while and feels a building within him, a feeling never known and it makes him quiver and tremble inside. Some stirring uncertainty. He watches Stevens's notebook slowly slide off his leg and onto the floor. Stevens doesn't seem to notice, he just sits there looking out the window. Seth picks up the phone and dials his mother's number.

HOBOKEN, NEW JERSEY
UNITED STATES

He has to kick the door open at the top of the stairwell and he stumbles out onto the roof, face contorted in something like agony or despair or fear, his cheeks wet with tears, snot running into his mouth. Little choking sounds come out of his throat, whimperings and groans.

The morning sky is the same—the same as the one in the dream. He tries to look up at it and let out a scream at the undulating mass of faces he sees there, but the sound won't come, just more whimpering breath. He chokes on the air and stares. After a few moments, he shudders and tries to move away, to break his gaze from the sky, the sky too large now, the sky within him too. It's hard for him to walk across the surface of the roof; the building seems to move and shift beneath him and still he moans in despair, in confusion. The sky rolls outward above and he tries to not look at it, helpless not to. Across the river the city burns. Somewhere below in the streets he hears a bubbling sound like light—a child's laughter, other enchanted voices. In three shaky strides he makes it to the edge and, blubbering uncontrollably now, contorts his shivering body over the brick parapet and falling, falls, to darkness.

LANZHOU, GANSU PROVINCE
CHINA

She begins the article with a proper lead.

Mass hallucinations may have affected a large portion of the populace in Gansu province, according to the Chinese Minister of Health, Shi Zhiming.

But the reporter doesn't feel good about it. Her supervisor, Lu, told her to type it up immediately for release over the wires, the wires buzzing with incoming stories, with pleas for help. She has five minutes to write the article.

Zhiming reported at a brief press conference this morning that the incident could be a possible critical situation for the government in Beijing.

She turns from the computer and rereads the facts Lu gave her on a piece of pink paper. Before dawn this morning several families had called on local physicians at the small town outside of Lanzhou regarding a similar dream that had woken them all up. Within an hour of sunrise, nearly the entire town had congregated at the central fountain. Minister Zhiming was notified immediately by the doctors in the area.

But, the reporter thinks, *Zhiming was also contacted by every single province and town and city in the whole country with the same symptoms. Why is only Lanzhou to be mentioned? What about the rest of the world? Who will care about a wire report from a small, rural newspaper?* The three dead bodies she saw at the side of the road are still in her mind. An entire family.

According to the physician reports faxed to the Minister's office this morning, most people of the village of Lanzhou had woken up at nearly the same time having experienced a similar dream.

Lu won't like my story construction, she thinks to herself. *He'll want me to take out all the references to the dream. He told me not to mention it.* The reporter looks down at her list of quotes from the press conference that occurred only moments before and winces. Her hands itch above the keys. She knows what she wants to write. Her brother had called and told about the chaos, the fires and death and chaos in the cities. All over the world a change, and an encompassing peacefulness too, a sense that now, finally, everything is connected—though a horror for some. She grits her teeth for a few moments and looks at the clock. Sweat trickles down her torso and she begins to type.

Incidents of mass hallucinations are rare but can occur, according to Zhiming. When asked about the possible nature of the incidents he said that mass hallucinations are "usually associated with the unconscious. This occurs when the hidden desires of a person, or an entire populace, manifest themselves in reality."

She's supposed to cite some of the better examples of mass hallucination, noting that most individuals involved merely see something that isn't there, such as a UFO or a ghost. *Not addressing the fact that everyone was asleep at the time will bring more attention to it*, she thinks to herself with a smile. Lu and her bosses are idiots.

They also want her to write about how a drug or chemical is usually to blame for mass hallucinations. It's so unbelievably ridiculous.

"The water and food sources of Gansu are being collected and tested as we speak," said Zhiming. He cited a number of hallucinogenic or otherwise toxic substances that might produce a similar effect upon a populace. "A chemical, maybe a fungus of some kind, is most likely the culprit," he concluded.

The reporter sighs. Lu will come bustling in at any moment to take the story. She prints it out and tries to call her brother back but there's no signal on her cellphone. It's deadened. Then the computer flutters, goes blue. All the lights flicker and die. The printer stops mid-page. It's silent now in the corridor outside her office.

The reporter sits back in darkness and smiles to herself. She didn't sleep last night because she had to work. She didn't have the dream. Maybe now she will get her chance.

NOGALES, SONORA
MEXICO

They walk slowly through the litter-strewn desert with faint smiles across their features, along a narrow path lined with gangly shrubs greening and cacti plump from a recent rain. Below them are what shacks remain across the slum-covered hillsides descending into the smoldering heart of the city. Every once in a while, the path narrows too much and the old man steps aside and gingerly lets her pass ahead while holding back some branch and she always thanks him, blushing, and he always says, "No ai de que." The clouds hang heavy on the jagged horizon, looming over the mountains where the sun has just hidden for the day, ablazened now and tinged with burnt umber, the faintest pink edge, promising more color to come. The very air is tinctured and sweet and the cicadas buzz mechanically all around them but fall silent when they get too close.

They don't say much, just little mumbling things about how quiet the streets are already or how the fires in the city had died down so quickly or whether they'll make it before the sun goes down. At one point she says that she wishes they'd done this more often. He tells her they would from now on.

At the top of a small rise, they look at one another and stop. There's a small clearing of gravelly ground and he spreads the blanket he's carried and they sit down and sip from a bottle of water and watch the sky. They still don't speak but eventually, as the clouds turn brilliant with luscious reds, he reaches over and takes her hand in his and she returns the gentle pressure of his flesh on hers. It is the first time they've touched each other in any intimate way, their first touch as lovers. And they simply sit there, occasionally looking at one another, whether the look is returned or not—sit there and watch the weather and descending light. The cloud grows dark in the center, heralding night's approach, and the buzzing cries of the cicadas die off one by one.

"Esperanza," he says and his voice sounds strange in the accumulating silence. "What do you think about it?" Her white hair flutters in an unfelt breeze. She finally turns to face him and he feels warmed—her face among so many others.

"Well, we've always been together, in a way, but—"

"But like this? And after all this time…"

"It had to take this long," she says and sighs. "Maybe there had to be enough of us, enough of us secretly wishing such a thing."

"Yes, but so many people died," he mutters, throwing a pebble at nothing. "And not just the ones that didn't understand, the ones that couldn't take it all." He shivers, recalling what he had seen earlier in the day. "There were innocents."

"There will always be innocents," she says through a sigh. "Maybe, I don't know, but maybe it was God's will and it had to be done." She turns and smiles at his questioning face. "All of us refused to put up with it any more…any more meanness, any more…"

"But God's will?" he asks, shifting uncomfortably. He hasn't really heard that expression since his only son was killed so many years ago. It holds a certain emptiness.

"Maybe we are all God, Paulo. All of us that ever have been or will be. It was *our* dream."

And her words send a shiver through his once tired body, the possible truth of them. A cloud hangs heavy in the sky and darkens. He smiles at it. "La vida es un sueño," he sings with a lightness in his chest. "Do you think it will come again, the dream?"

"Does it have to?" She says at the sky.

PERMISSIONS

Twister Poem Text (from page 123)

If you glanced up at the right moment you might think you had a
                    dust speck in your eye,
or perhaps a nervous tic, because you thought you'd seen a little
                    flicker in the cloud
that was building in the springtime sky and you'd go about your
                    business without a
second glance. But you'd be wrong. The flicker, quicker than you'd
                    imagine
possible, would transform itself into a little twirling spinning top
                    in the
center of the cloud, the balance point on which it stood resting on
the unseen floor that held the cloud in place. And if you'd kept
watching you would have seen the spinning spiral lengthen
until it reached all
the way from
heaven to
unsuspecting
earth
as if it was
reluctant
to move
but was
being
pulled
along
by the cloud
gathering
speed as
it looked
for somewhere
where it could clear
a convenient place
on which it could spread its
aching twisted limbs so they could pull their punches, finally fall-
                    ing asleep on a dusty
sofa, leaving disoriented, dislocated folk to mourn lost harvests,
                    homes—heartbreak.